Three Hours Late

Nicole
TROPE

Three Hours Late

ALLEN&UNWIN
SYDNEY•MELBOURNE•AUCKLAND•LONDON

First published in 2013

Copyright © Nicole Trope 2013

Allen & Unwin
83 Alexander Street
Crows Nest NSW 2065
Australia
Phone: (61 2) 8425 0100
Email: info@allenandunwin.com
Web: www.allenandunwin.com

Cataloguing-in-Publication details are available
from the National Library of Australia
www.trove.nla.gov.au

ISBN 978 1 74331 315 2

Set in 12/18 pt Minion Pro by Bookhouse, Sydney
Printed and bound in Australia by Griffin Press

10 9 8 7 6 5 4 3 2 1

MIX
Paper from
responsible sources
FSC
www.fsc.org FSC® C009448

The paper in this book is FSC® certified. FSC® promotes environmentally responsible, socially beneficial and economically viable management of the world's forests.

For Mom, Dad, Lyn and Elwin—my personal
cheerleading squad

In dreams there are flashes of his face.

Kaleidoscope light touches his hair.

His arms reach out.

In dreams his hand touches mine.

We twirl and dance touched by light and shade, spinning

until we cannot be seen.

Three hours late

'Aiden, we've been around this block twice already. Don't you think that if the guy was here we would've found him?' asked Julie.

'I know, I know,' said Aiden. 'But it just feels . . . I can't explain it, Jules. Maybe it's a little of that police instinct we're all supposed to have. Besides, the last call he made came from this tower.'

'Yeah, but that was an hour ago. The choppers have been over this park at least twice. They would've seen the car if he was here. Let's go check out some of the shopping centres. He told his wife he'd taken the kid to an arcade earlier today. Maybe he went back there. Shopping centres are a great place to hide. Let's start at the first one we come to and go from there. We're wasting time here.'

'I don't know, Jules. I think this guy will be closer to home.'

Julie pushed some blonde curls back behind her ear. 'I think he's hidden away in the dark somewhere far from prying eyes, just like the rat he is.'

'Don't make me pull rank, Jules,' said Aiden.

Julie and Aiden hadn't been partners long but they had clicked from the beginning. Julie never needed to be told who was in charge.

Now she looked at Aiden, hurt by the rebuke, but relaxed when she saw he was smiling.

'Fine, but this is the last time, okay? Go around once more and then we'll start on the shopping centres.'

The police cruiser crawled past the park again.

'I know it looks deserted but I just want to check out the bush at the back,' said Aiden. He pulled off the road into the dust and stone area that served as a car park and the two police officers climbed out of the car. In the dying light of the afternoon the empty swing moved back and forth as if waiting for a small body and pumping legs. The slight creak of the metal chains sent a shiver down Julie's spine. Even as a kid she'd never been a fan of the park. There were too many big kids, too many unknowns.

'There's nothing here,' said Julie, wrapping her arms around herself.

'Looks that way,' said Aiden. The bushland surrounding the park looked undisturbed.

•

White lines chased each other around the freshly marked oval. There were three schools close by that were probably getting ready for their sports carnivals. Aiden glanced across the empty stone steps that served as stands for watching parents. He didn't understand his certainty that the guy was here. It would be a stupid place to hide. It was too close to the house where the kid lived. The guy was probably hiding out in a giant car park where he would be almost impossible to find. Or maybe just maybe he was long gone by now. He could be on the highway heading out of Sydney on the way to Queensland. Or he could be hiding out in some small country town already. He could be anywhere.

'So why do I think he's here?' muttered Aiden.

He closed his eyes and tried to work out what was bothering him. He felt like there was something he was missing. But whatever it was it remained out of reach. He opened his eyes with a sigh.

The park had a small play area off to the side but was dominated by the oval in the middle. All around houses stood on sentry duty in the quiet Saturday afternoon. It was a little cold now for kids to be out but even so the park was eerily empty.

He turned to walk back to the car as the sun dipped a little lower on the horizon and then he caught something in his peripheral vision. He turned around and waited for it again.

And there it was: a flash as the last rays of the sun hit something metal. There *was* something in the bush.

Aiden started walking towards the place where he'd seen the flash. Crossing the oval, he noticed tyre tracks. He broke into a run.

He knew what he would find when he got to the cluster of gum trees, banksias and tangled undergrowth. He knew they would be there.

As he drew closer he saw the outline of the car, a blue Toyota sedan. He knew that when he checked the licence plate it would be WVX 217.

His heart was pumping now and despite the cold he was beginning to sweat. He slowed down and made himself a cat. If they were still in the car he didn't want to startle the man into doing anything stupid, and if they were outside the car he didn't want to alert the guy to his presence.

He crept forward, trying to avoid hidden twigs; cursing the gold-red fall of leaves that carpeted the ground.

The car's engine was running, just purring gently. Aiden wondered how long it had been running for. How long could a tank of petrol last if the car was parked?

He grabbed his taser from its holder. A gun would freak the kid out but he wouldn't know what a taser was.

He stepped forward and peered through the rear window.

When he couldn't see anything he moved around to one of the back passenger windows.

If the kid was in the back seat Aiden would have to signal to him to keep quiet. He already had his finger against his lips. Hopefully the kid would be more curious than terrified by the sight of a police officer looking through his window.

The man would probably be in the front seat and wouldn't see him. Unless of course they were both in the front seat and neither was in a position to see him. Unless neither of them was in a position to see anything.

Aiden looked back at the oval and saw Julie jogging across to meet him. He put his hand up, indicating that she should stop; the last thing he needed was more noise. Julie obliged and became a statue. She wouldn't move again until he told her to.

He refocused on the window. He saw a booster seat covered in pictures of Winnie-the-Pooh and his friends. Eeyore stared out the window at Aiden, his tail drooping and face resigned. There was no sign of the boy.

The park and the car sat together in the silence of the day. Aiden stepped forward again, straining his muscles to keep his body light on the ground. Holding his breath, he looked into the front seat.

He put his taser back into its holder.

He stood up straight and waved at Julie.

She resumed her run across the oval.

1

Liz watched Alex make his way up the front path.

His progress was visible from the living room window with only a slight twitch of the curtains.

Alex stood deliberately on every crack he saw, sometimes moving to the other side of the path to make sure he didn't miss one.

His hair was slicked down with water and even from her position at the window she could see he was freshly shaved.

Once, so very long ago, she had watched him like this when he came to pick her up for a date.

Then she had watched him with the delicious anticipation of the night ahead. She would stand at the window with her heart hammering and her cheeks burning, just waiting for him to ring the bell. Her hair would be perfectly curled and styled and her toes would already be pinched by her too-high heels. Her body would react to his presence even before she looked into his eyes. Her stomach fluttered and burned with infatuation and desire. She would watch him walk up the front path and think, 'This must be love.'

It had been love.

Once it had been love.

Now she watched him to gauge his mood, to figure out what her best opening line would be. Now her stomach burned with dread.

This morning she was wearing an old maternity tracksuit and her hair was pulled back with odd-coloured clips. Her breath still smelled of her breakfast coffee.

She hoped he would not want to look at her. She hoped he would simply take his son and leave. Today, she needed him to see only that she was unkempt and ugly. 'Don't look at me!' she wanted to yell.

Logically she knew that she could have been dressed in a garbage bag and there would still be no way he would just leave without forcing her to make herself understood again. No way would he just take Luke and go. Logically she knew that, but she also knew that when it came to Alex, the rules of the universe only applied sometimes. So this morning she had nursed her cup of coffee and prayed, because you never know your luck.

But now that she had seen him she knew he would want to stay. The dark green shirt he was wearing still held traces of crisp fold lines from when he had bought it. Liz had never seen it before. He would want to talk. He would not let her off lightly. Not after last night.

Shit—last night.

Liz didn't want to think about last night. She wasn't ready to deal with her mistake but Alex would not be dismissed. She could see from the way he walked and the way he dressed that he believed something had changed last night.

In the morning light that was always so cruel she would have to make the facts clear again. She would have to tell him yet again that their marriage was finished.

She watched as he smoothed his hair down and then, just before he lifted his hand to ring the bell, she stepped forward to open the door.

He smiled when he saw her.

She looked down at her cold bare feet. Her nail polish was mostly chipped away.

It was a charming smile. It included his eyes and encouraged a return gesture.

Liz looked up but stared past him.

'Hi,' she said.

He nodded in reply.

Liz angled her body away from him and called, 'Luke, Daddy's here. Come on—get your backpack.'

'Daddy, Daddy, yay, yay!' Luke yelled from the other room.

Liz knew that Luke would leave the television on and dart into the living room and it was possible that in the chaos of his excited greeting Alex would forget about Liz and just leave with his son.

'That's right, Daddy's here. Come on, don't keep him waiting. You and Daddy are going to have so much fun.'

'Yeah, me and Dad are gonna have fun! Hey, Dad, what did you bring me?'

Liz rubbed her hands through her son's fine blond hair, smoothing it back off his face. His eyes were lit up with the joy of seeing his father, his arms already outstretched in anticipation of a hug.

'Ah, it's in the car, little man, but can you give me a minute? I just need to talk to Mum about something.'

It was possible he would just leave, but it was not probable.

'Do we have to do this now, Alex?' She said. She made sure her voice was light and high. She made sure to keep out any note of impatience. It was his choice to make after all. It was always his choice. But which choice would he make? Who was Alex today? Which Alex was standing in front of her in his crisp new shirt? Liz rubbed at her bunched neck muscles.

After his greeting smile his face had set to neutral, hiding his mood. Her stomach churned and she recognised a feeling she had put aside in the last few months, except when she was talking to him. It came rushing back now, closing in on her.

His eyes narrowed. 'Yes, we do need to do it now. Go and find Nana, Luke. Mum and I need to talk.'

Luke heard the catch in his father's voice but he was only three. He hadn't yet learned when to keep quiet.

'But, Dad . . .'

Liz jumped in quickly when she saw Alex's eyes flash. He had never hurt Luke, never even laid a hand on him, but she could foresee a time when the boy would be a continual challenge to his father, and then who knew what would happen?

Alex didn't like to be challenged.

'It's okay, Luke. Do what Dad says. Go and find Nana. And your blankie, Luke—don't forget your blankie.'

'Why does he need to drag that thing around, Liz? He's three years old already. Isn't it time he gave it up?'

'I think he's been through a lot, Alex. His blanket is his security.'

'He wouldn't need it anymore if his whole life hadn't been thrown into chaos.'

And behind those words were so many years of blame that Liz didn't even need to acknowledge them. Instead she dipped her head a little and weaselled her way out of the confrontation.

'Just give him a few more months and we'll sort it out, Alex.

He's only a little boy.' She was aware that her voice had taken on a pleading whine. She hated the way she sounded.

Alex shook his head at her and stood up straighter, nearly reaching her height. He could always tell when he had the upper hand.

'So what did you want to discuss?' she said, buying time to allow herself a moment to try and find the right words to appease him. She needed words that would keep him calm and words that would help her maintain her distance. Her head filled up with white noise. There were no right words.

'You know what I want to discuss, babe. I want to talk about last night.'

Now his voice had an edge of sexual fire. The tone crept inside her, warming her whole body.

Her cheeks flushed. She was mortified by last night. If only because of the way her body responded. If only because of the way her body responded right now, clinging to the memory. It was treason.

She sighed, wondering if it would be better just to say that last night had made everything all right and they were going to be one big happy family again. She knew she could pacify him now and then get her father to come over and explain the facts again when Luke was due to be dropped home. Alex understood her father's size and the possibility of him using his fists. Liz had thought about calling in her father more than once, more than ten times, but she never had.

Jack Searle towered above Alex and Liz could see Alex diminished every time they were in the same room. But Jack didn't like to use his fists; he sank into silence instead. He simply left the wife he couldn't deal with. He just left and though Liz felt, even now, that she would never recover from being discarded like that along with her mother, she knew there were worse things you could do than just leave.

She thought hard about what she could say to Alex now but her mind was stubbonly blank. She had to be conciliatory but firm at the same time. She needed to keep him happy but make herself clear. Talking to Alex was exhausting.

Liz realised she should just have left it to her mother to hand Luke over to Alex. She should have stayed in bed until she had figured out what to say to him. She had been doing that for months already—being somewhere else when he came to pick up Luke—so why had she opened the door for him today?

She tried to find some placating words, but the small part of her that was recovering from being married to him took over her mouth and she said, 'Oh, Alex, last night was a mistake. It was nothing. I'm sorry I let it go so far, but you have to know that there's really nothing to discuss.'

'I don't know that, Liz. It was not nothing. I'm not nothing.' Alex bit down on his lip. He knew her mother was in the house.

Then he rubbed his eyes and took a deep breath. 'We were so good together,' he said, bringing out his smile again. 'Surely you can see that. We were always so good together.'

She shook her head and looked at her feet again. The nail polish had been a bright blue. It was called Caribbean Dream.

Alex changed tack. 'Come on, babe, give it another go. I can have you and Luke back home and unpacked in an hour. It will be so good for him to have us together again.'

His voice was warm and smooth like melted chocolate. She hated what he became when they discussed the possibility of getting back together again. She hated the way he darted back and forth between charm and aggression. She knew how quickly it could all go back the way it had been. In darker moments, when she thought her future would be spent in her mother's house watching the world go by and waiting for her son to grow up, she had to force herself to acknowledge what would happen—after a few honeymoon days—if she returned.

She had to remember how much it hurt to be hit with an open hand and a closed fist and how hard it was to always be trying to figure out the right thing to say. She was always on guard. Even in her sleep she had needed to be vigilant, worrying through her fitful dreams about accidently waking him. Now she only felt like that when he came over to see Luke.

'Alex, I can't talk about this now. I have things to do and you don't have much time today. He needs to be back by two.'

Alex's brown eyes darkened almost to black.

'You can be such a bitch, Elizabeth. I'm not going to let you just dismiss me. I know what I felt last night wasn't just me.'

Liz felt the sting of the word 'bitch'. The part of her that had recovered a little from being with Alex, the Liz who wanted to step out of the shadows, opened her mouth. She hated being called by her full name.

'God, Alex, leave it alone, will you. You got what you wanted last night but it was a one-time thing. It won't happen again. I was just . . .'

'You were just what?'

'Lonely, I guess. I was just lonely.'

'I can change that, babe. I've been lonely too and I can make sure that you never feel that way again. We can do it, Liz. We can try again.'

'We're better apart than together, Alex. Please, let's just not discuss this now.'

'I can change, Liz. If you just give me a chance I can do better.'

'You always say that, Alex. Every time it happens you tell me it won't happen again, but it keeps happening. Maybe you need to take some time out and get some help.'

'Fuck that, Liz. I don't need some shrink telling me what's wrong with me.'

Liz had heard it all before—once, twice, two hundred times.

Every now and again he would agree to go to counselling and then back out at the last minute, claiming it was all 'just bullshit about what your mother did wrong, and you and I both know I never had a mother for most of my life'. His mother's desertion was his favourite excuse for his behaviour, and his last resort when he wanted Liz's sympathy. 'My mother left when I was five. One day I went to school and when I got home she was gone and I've never seen her again.'

'Look, Alex, we'll talk later, okay? Just bring him home at two and I'll put him down for his nap and we can talk.'

'Can we talk about getting back together? Can we talk about ending this bullshit?'

'Look . . . just . . . we'll talk, okay?'

'Yeah, we'll talk, but it'll be about what you want. It's always about what you want. I'm not some boy you can lead around by the nose, Liz.'

'Please, Alex . . . not again.'

Alex clenched his fists and Liz could see that even standing at the front door of her mother's house she was still not safe. His silent fury filled up the space between them. Liz felt it choke her and she slowly moved one foot back so that she could turn and run.

Luke came bounding back into the room then. A puppy full of bounce.

Suddenly there was more light and Liz felt like she could fill her lungs again.

'Is it time to go, Dad? Are you done? Can we go, Mum? Can we go, Dad? Let's go, Dad, let's go!'

'We're done,' said Liz, and she looked only at Luke.

'Bye, Mum.'

'Bye, Luke. Give me a kiss.'

'Nah, kisses are squishy.'

'Okay . . . no squishy kisses. How about a hug?'

''Kay. Love you, Mum.'

'Love you, Luke.' She turned to Alex. 'Have him back by two, please.'

Liz watched Alex.

'Maybe today's not the best day for you two to go out,' she said.

'Awww . . . Mum,' said Luke.

'We're going out. Just Luke and me—two boys out on the town,' said Alex and his voice had relaxed again.

Luke giggled.

'Well just . . . just call me if you need me, okay,' she said.

Alex made no reply.

'Bye, Mum, love you, Mum, bye, Mum.'

Liz waved then closed the door on Alex and his sad accusing stare. She wanted him gone and now he was gone.

She felt a surge of triumph. She had stood her ground. She had not been pushed into saying something that she would regret.

•

'Standing your ground' was one of the first things Rebecca tried to teach them.

Rebecca was the psychologist in charge of the sad little group that Liz attended once a week. Thursdays from ten am to twelve pm—coffee and tea provided. There she sat in a circle with all the other bruised and broken women trying to find a way out of the lives they had somehow stumbled into.

Rebecca liked to make them stamp their feet and shout 'no' to show them all that they had the strength and the power to defend themselves. They stamped and shouted as loud as they could, laughing and enjoying their raised voices. But they were stamping and shouting at each other in the safe confines of the group. Outside the group it was an entirely different story.

'If you can just change the way you respond to the abuser you have a chance to change your relationship. If you can stand your ground in a safe environment where you have others around to protect you, you can force the abuser to see you as a person who has their own power,' Rebecca said.

'What crap,' Glenda said. 'That'll just make him more pissed off than before. Then he'll lie awake at night trying to figure out how to slit my throat.'

'Obviously you have to make a decision based on your own individual circumstances,' said Rebecca.

'Yeah,' laughed Glenda. 'Our own individual circumstances. Individually, each and every one of us is a bit fucked.'

Liz had only gone to the community centre because her mother insisted. The ad for the domestic violence support group had been up on the noticeboard right outside the shopping centre. It was next to an ad for lessons on flower arranging, like there was a choice. Her mother had pointed it out.

'Just give it a couple of goes, Liz. You never know—it might help.'

Liz just sniffed. 'I don't need to witter on about what Alex did. I've left him, haven't I?'

'Liz, he was here nearly every day last week. You may have moved out but you definitely haven't left him.'

'Like you would know.'

Ellen had sighed. 'You need to do something, Liz, so go or I'm giving your father a call and he can figure out what to do about Alex.'

'Aren't I too old to be treated like a child?'

'You're never too old to be treated with concern, Liz. You need to talk to someone.'

Liz took down the number and shoved it into her bag where it stayed for weeks. She waited for her mother to just drop the issue but Ellen was surprisingly dogmatic about her getting some help.

'I never got any help after your father left and I'm not saying this is the same thing but you can't hide from your pain, Liz. I did it and basically checked out for years after he left. I know I did.'

Liz didn't say anything. She waited for her mother to finish talking.

'Thanks for agreeing with me, my darling,' said Ellen.

'What exactly would you like me to say? Do you want me to say it didn't happen? Because we both know it did.'

'Liz, I can apologise all I like but I can't give you back those years. So all I can do is try to prevent you from making the same mistakes. You have Luke to think about and I know you want to do better than I did. You need help. You need to talk to other women and try to figure out how to move your relationship past the point where he has any hold over you.'

'Like Alcoholics Anonymous but for domestic abuse?'

'Yes,' laughed Ellen. 'Like that.'

•

After she heard the car start up Liz leaned her head against the front door. If she was honest with herself, she knew that she hadn't really achieved anything.

All the voices ran round and round in her head and it was getting harder to know who she should listen to. This morning she had managed to keep some control of the situation, but she knew that when Alex brought Luke back this afternoon he would find a way to make her feel like it was her fault he raised his hands to her. Her fault they were unhappy, her fault they were shuffling Luke between the two of them.

Her mother and father believed it was her fault for staying, Alex believed it was her fault for leaving, and the only thing Liz really knew for sure was that it was all her fault.

Scenes from the night before flashed through her mind again, forcing her to shut her eyes and wish them away. Things had been getting better. It had been easier to keep Alex at a distance. He was responding to emails, accepting that she would leave messages for him rather than speak to him, and the conversations about their failed marriage had been getting shorter. But then there was last night.

And Liz knew, with the same intuition that told her when she was going to be hurt, that last night had made things worse. She could see herself at the bottom of the hill and she didn't know if she had the strength to push the rock all the way to the top once more.

2

Afterwards she had twisted herself up in her sheets for hours cursing her stupidity. There was no way she should have let it happen but the tender touch of his hands was the one thing she did miss about him. They could be gentle, those hands; they could be so many other things, but they could also be gentle.

He had called late in the afternoon, 'I want to come over and kiss Luke goodnight. I want to do the whole bath time and story thing. Is that okay with you?'

His voice was so soft, so sad, that it broke her heart. He was asking to see his son. He wasn't ranting or demanding, he was just asking.

•

'Stay away from the abuser as much as possible,' said Rebecca. 'Avoid the places he goes and the friends he likes to hang out with.'

'How can I stay away?' asked Liz. It was the first time she had opened her mouth. 'He has to see his son. How can I stay away when I have to keep inviting him in?'

'You have to get a lawyer and tell the police,' said Rebecca.

'And then?' asked Liz.

'And then you'll still have to let the bastard see the kid because he's never laid a hand on him and fathers have rights, don'tcha know,' said Rhonda, who had been in the group for a whole year and still hadn't worked out how to maintain a proper distance from the love of her life, who liked to hit when he'd had a few.

Liz nodded at what Rhonda had said and in that moment accepted what she already knew to be true. She and Alex were tied together forever.

They were tied together by Luke.

•

'Can I come over, Liz—please?'

That voice made her weak. It brought back the way he would curl up next to her and plead, 'Don't ever leave me, Liz, don't ever leave,' like a little boy.

The voice tugged at her. He sounded so alone and one word from her could change that—for one night at least.

She had promised to stay forever. High on his adoration she would have agreed to anything, and now she had left and made him sad. She understood his despair was her fault. She had left to save herself but he couldn't see that. He seemed genuinely bewildered by her behaviour.

So when she had heard that voice, the voice that drew her in and softened her heart, Liz couldn't say no.

It was just story time and bath time. It was a reasonable request, wasn't it? He was always exhorting her to be reasonable. 'Look at it from my point of view, Liz. You have to see that this cannot be just about me.' The trouble was that when she did look at it from his point of view she forgot her own perspective. Alex was very good at making her brush her own feelings aside.

But he had called and asked so politely, so softly and so sadly, that she forgot to think about herself. All she thought was, 'He's a good dad and he just wants to see his kid.' She ignored the voice inside that told her to protect the small steps she had taken with boundaries and limitations, and gave in again.

'Sure,' she said. 'My mum will be out with friends so I guess I could use the help.'

•

Her therapy group was filled with women who took two steps forward and three steps back.

Sometimes they laughed about that over coffee and cigarettes. It was good to have a laugh. They turned away bruised faces and held their cups carefully with broken wrists and laughed. Rhonda thought it was something chemical. 'It's like they change the way our brains work as soon as we're around them. We know that if we could just stay away it would be better for everyone, but then they come over and you can't stop them from seeing their kids. They come over and their voices get low and soft and maybe it's a smell or something but we can't help ourselves.'

The other women nodded in agreement. You could get addicted to that small flip of your heart, to that warmth between your legs when they came near you. You could get as addicted as the poor sad bloke on a bench with a bottle of cheap whisky for breakfast.

'There should be a special clinic we can go where they wean us off them,' Liz said and Glenda had laughed so much she spilled her coffee.

•

'Great, I'll see you soon,' Alex had replied.

He had turned up right on time as he had always done and Luke's eyes were the best reward for any stupid choices she made.

'My dad's here, Mum, my dad's here! Did you see him, Mum? My dad's here! Mummy, Mummy, Mum, Mum.'

Bath time became an adventure and three stories had to be read and Liz felt her heart break just a little at the thought of how Luke would ask for his father the next day.

She had explained it carefully. She had explained it the way the psychologist had told her to explain it, but Luke still couldn't quite understand.

'But why can't Dad live with us at Nana's house?'

'Just because, Luke.'

'Because why?'

'Luke, it's time for bed,' she would say, or, 'How about we play a game?' or 'Let's go and get a treat,' because she couldn't tell him the truth. It was not a truth anyone would ever want to hear.

Luke knew something. He had seen things and even though he couldn't yet connect the dots he did know that there were reasons why his mother and father lived apart. It didn't stop him wanting them back together, of course. Liz was an adult with a child of her own and she still sometimes fantasised about a reunion for her own parents.

Liz watched Alex read to Luke and her heart was stung by the loss of the possibility of a picture-perfect family. They sat together on the bed and Luke was all warm and sleepy and Alex had his head on the pillow and she could see the colour Luke's hair would become as he got older. Liz had seen pictures of Alex at the same age and it was difficult to tell the difference between them. Luke looked so like his father it was funny. Same nose, same chin, same smile.

It was like a scene from a movie. It was a scene from a postcard. Somewhere inside, she wanted it to last forever.

'My boys,' she thought, and she should have known right then and there just to shut down, but it was hard always being on the lookout. It took work to maintain distance and repress emotions.

'Do you want a drink?' she asked when Luke's thumb was firmly in his mouth, his blankie held tightly in his other hand.

•

'Don't encourage them to stay after they've seen the children,' Rebecca said, and all the women in the group had looked around the room or at the back wall where happy family paintings from the preschool covered the bricks.

'Sometimes there's stuff to fix,' said Rhonda.

'Yeah, you need a man around the house every now and again,' said Glenda.

'It doesn't matter,' said Rebecca. 'Say goodbye and show them to the door. Don't let them stay, don't give them the chance.'

•

Some nights the loneliness sucked Liz into an abyss and she had to lie on her hands, knowing that if she just picked up the phone he would come running and he would put his arms around her and chase the shadows away.

'Yeah . . . yeah sure, a drink would be good. Wine if you've got some.'

He didn't say, 'Why now when you've been such a bitch?' and he didn't say, 'I have better things to do and other people to see,' and he didn't say, 'I think we should keep things simple right now until the divorce is finalised.' He didn't even give her a questioning look. He smiled at her like he had been waiting for the invitation and let her lead the way and she forgot herself. She forgot everything.

She had poured red wine and made pasta and afterwards she wished that her mother had arrived home earlier.

They sat in dim light in the lounge room and talked about Luke and how cute he was and how funny he was and what they thought he would be when he grew up.

They opened a second bottle of wine and watched the fire, built properly by Alex the way she and her mother could never build it, and she had felt her skin glow with pleasure. This was how it was supposed to be.

They ate and drank and laughed and all through it her own little voice was trying to get her attention. But the Alex that she had fallen in love with was on show and he was hard to resist.

They cleared the dishes and when he kissed her she knew she could stop him but that old chemical reaction came back and when he touched her breasts she was lost. The room was in a light spin and the pasta sat heavily in her stomach and her limbs slid down to the floor.

It was her fault. Even as it was happening she knew she was letting it happen, she knew that.

When it was over Alex had curled his body around hers and stroked her hair while he talked, and she listened.

'God, I've missed you, Liz. I've missed us so much. We need to be a family again. We're so good together. You can see that, can't you?'

They were lying on the floor of the kitchen and the cold from the slate tiles was beginning to seep into her skin.

Regret was a stone on her chest.

'Alex, I think . . . I think . . .' She got up and pulled on her clothes, smoothing her long black hair back into its neat ponytail.

'Don't think, my love. You think too much. Just come home and bring my boy back. Just let us be a family again.'

'Alex, I'm sorry. I shouldn't have let this happen. Look, I think this was a mistake. We can't be together again, Alex. We're better off apart. It's better for Luke. You have to see that.' She crossed her arms over her chest for protection and backed away.

He stepped forward, forcing her to step back against a wall.

'The worst marriage is better than the best divorce, Liz. We'll scar him for life. How come you can't see that? He'll grow up the same way we did. Didn't we want better for him? Isn't that what we said? You need to come back home. You need to come back to me.'

'I can't, Alex. Please. I'm sorry about this but I just can't—I . . . I need more time.'

He nodded his head like it was the first time she had ever offered him that excuse. He knew what she was saying. He knew what she meant but he nodded his head as though he imagined that Liz would eventually have had enough time and she could then go back to being his wife and sharing a house and a bed with him. Liz smiled a little to convince him that what she said was true.

'Yeah, that's right, you need more time,' he said. 'Think it over tonight and we can talk when I pick Luke up tomorrow morning. I'm going crazy without my kid, Liz. I'm going crazy without you.'

'You go pretty crazy when we're there,' Liz thought, but she knew those words would never leave her mouth.

'Alex, it may not be the best id—'

'Fuck that, Liz. Fuck the best idea. I need you home. I need Luke with me. I need to see my child every day. He's my child, Liz. *Mine*. How would you feel if you couldn't see him every day? How the fuck would you feel?'

The wine had turned to acid in her stomach now and the nausea rose inside her.

'You can see him whenever you want to. You know that.'

'It's not the same, Liz. I want to be there all the time. This is killing me, you know. I sit at home and try to figure out how to make it right. How come you aren't doing the same thing? Don't you miss me?'

'I just think . . .'

'Spare me, Liz. I know what you think. Christ, you're so cold.' Alex took another step forward. He was close now, too close, but she could not get any further away from him.

'Nothing can touch you,' he hissed. 'I hope you never have to feel the pain I feel. I hope you never . . .'

And then the front door opened and her mother came in. Liz breathed a sigh of relief and moved across the room.

Her mother didn't greet Alex. She could not abide his presence in her house. It was the only thing her parents agreed on—Alex was the biggest mistake Liz had ever made.

But because of him there was Luke.

As far as Liz could see that ended the argument right there.

'It can't all be my fault, Liz,' Alex whispered to her when she walked him to the door. 'There's an old cliché about it taking two to tango and you know that you don't make things easy, Liz. You know it.'

Liz wanted to tell him that there was no excuse for where his anger took him but she had kept quiet instead. She had closed the door on him without defending herself, without saying anything else.

She had closed the door and hoped that her fuck-up would disappear with the night.

3

Ellen came into the room while Liz was still standing by the door. Liz knew that her mother had deliberately waited in the kitchen until Alex had left. She wondered how much Ellen had heard.

Liz knew that she had a fair idea what had happened last night. She had stayed in the living room while Liz saw Alex out and, even though Liz knew her mother was only protecting her, she couldn't help but feel like a guilty teenager.

'When are you going to let go properly, Liz?' she had asked as they switched off the lights on the way to bed.

'I have let go, Mum. He just came over to read a story to Luke and I made some dinner, it's no big deal.'

'Oh, Liz,' said her mother and shook her head.

Liz had turned away from her then and taken refuge in the shower, where she washed away Alex's smell and his touch. She scrubbed until her skin was pink with her resolutions for the future. She would not let this happen again.

For the first time, she had a strong desire to be in a place of her own.

She wanted to be free of being watched, of being judged. She always fell short of her mother's expectations or Alex's expectations. She wanted to be somewhere enclosed in her own silent space. If she had not had Luke she could have ended her marriage and gone away. She could have climbed on a plane and finally gone to England or Italy. She could have lost herself and her pain among strangers. If she had not had Luke.

But because she did have Luke she had no choice but to return home, and she knew that right there was part of the reason, a small part of the reason, that she had stayed with Alex so long. Each time she had pictured herself turning up on her mother's doorstep she had imagined the sting of humiliation she'd feel at being so wrong about her choices.

'I suppose you need to stay here,' her mother had said on that summer's day five months ago, forgoing a smile of welcome in favour of an 'I told you so'.

'It won't be for long,' she said.

'I'll just bet,' her mother answered. 'Come on, Lukie, let's go and get you settled. Now the blue room can really be your room.'

Her mother had warned her about Alex. 'It's just a feeling I have, Liz. The boy is too desperate to start a family. What kind of twenty-three-year-old man wants a baby?'

'Maybe one who won't fuck off the moment he meets a nice little blonde girl.'

'It doesn't get you anywhere, Liz, dragging me down. It doesn't get you anywhere. I know who I married but it doesn't mean every thought I have on the subject of men should be discounted. Marry Alex if you will, but I'm not sure he's the right man for you.'

Of course Liz had ignored her. Hadn't she been doing that since the day her father left? It had been so many years ago, but Liz could replay every detail in her head.

Her mother had nearly ripped the shirt off her father's back as he tried to leave. She had clung and wept and degraded herself. Her father had moved resolutely forward, packing his bag and getting into the truck and driving away.

Liz had never imagined that her father would run off with the chubby blonde waitress from the place he got his lunch. The woman was a sad cliché. She talked incessantly about everything and anything. Her balloon breasts puffed out of her low-cut top and her chunky legs were never helped by the length of her skirts. Liz couldn't fathom the attraction. Her father was not a fan of conversation in general.

On the day Jack left to live with 'that slut', Ellen had stood in the street, screaming and cursing. She had picked up some stones from the garden and thrown them at the truck as it roared away. One had bounced off the side, leaving a small dent in the face of a smiling piano. The neighbours had opened their doors and stood in silent condemnation before going back inside their houses away from the crazy woman shrieking in the street. Ellen had stood alone in the empty street watching the sun set and convulsively tearing at her clothes. She had returned to the house to find her tall, gawky daughter silent and horrified.

'I don't need your father's fucking face here right now,' Ellen had shouted. 'Just go to your room!'

Liz had never forgiven her. Initially she had blamed herself for her father leaving, but she soon decided her mother was the culprit.

Ellen lived her life perched on the edge of hysteria and Jack couldn't take it anymore. He was a quiet man who took up a lot of space. His hands spanned a dinner plate and his voice rumbled from deep inside his chest. He was, of all things, a piano mover. He had three trucks on the road and commanded a reasonable amount of respect in their neighbourhood. He'd been in all the big houses and met a few famous faces. Not that he ever discussed it.

As a child, Liz had gone with him once or twice when he went out to move the large, precious objects from one house to another.

'Oh, do be careful,' the owner would say as Jack and his men began shifting the piano.

'She'll be right, madam,' her father would say to the tense owner. 'Me an' the boys been doing this awhile. We know what's what.' The owner of the piano seemed grateful to be told to basically shut up.

And when the piano was safely in position in the new house the owner would virtually weep with gratitude. Liz had never understood the attachment to an inanimate object. It made music, but so what? She lived in a neighbourhood where getting the rent paid on time could be a major concern.

Her father did well and made money, invested in new trucks and more drivers. Who would have thought the world had so many pianos?

At night her father didn't go to the pub; he liked to drop his big frame into a chair and just sit. He didn't even need to watch TV, but he liked the country music channel, filled as it was with the sweet voices of the hard-done-by. By the end of the day he was worn out from keeping up the weight of the pianos and his client's expectations. Ellen clung and whined and Liz had moments where she followed suit, having only her mother's behaviour as a reference.

Liz's mother wanted to do things, see things, go places. She wanted to move to a bigger house and buy a nicer car and go on holiday.

'What's the point in making money if all you do is sink it back into the business?'

'Why can't we have a holiday? It's not as if you don't have Scott to run things for a week or two.'

'Tell me about your day, Jack—who did you see? Did you see anyone famous?'

'Please, Jack, you can't just sit there like a lump of lard. Get up, for God's sake, and let's go out somewhere. Let's go to dinner. I am so sick of being shut up in this house all day.'

On the day he left to 'shack up with his little blonde whore', Ellen had mixed some whisky with Diet Coke and been rewarded with the joyful vengeance alcohol allowed her to feel. From then on she woke each day and counted the hours until she could drink again. She dived straight into the whisky bottle and, while she maintained the bitter facade of the dignified divorcee in public, she was incapable of truly functioning for years.

Liz hated her father for leaving, but she understood.

Each time her father came home for an access visit Liz would watch her mother humiliate herself afresh. She would begin, dressed up and drenched in scent, with sexy cajoling and end up crying and spitting venom. Eventually Liz's father got his daughter a mobile phone so he could ring her to announce his arrival without having to enter the house.

Liz pushed against her father's union with all the might of her teenage years, but after spending enough time with her father and his waitress, Liz realised that her father had finally found his perfect match. Lilly talked nonstop but her father didn't talk back. He didn't have to. She did enough talking for the two of them and she didn't seem to need him to answer her questions; she just needed someone to talk at. Liz decided her father must see it as pleasant background noise, something to listen to while he sat. Lilly went out with her friends, sold Tupperware, played bingo at the local church and read to the blind on Tuesday afternoons. She was constantly busy and didn't seem to mind whether Liz's father was home or not.

To a teenage Liz, this had seemed like the secret to a good marriage—not actually needing the other person. But Liz didn't mind being needed; in fact, she quite liked it. If you were needed you could never just be left behind.

It never occurred to her that her mother had once been a young bride blind to her husband's faults.

Liz could not imagine that her mother had chosen to ignore or misinterpret the things that niggled at her when she was dating her future husband; just as she herself had ignored the signs when she and Alex were dating.

As a young bride Ellen had mistaken her husband's reticence for deep thought and his lack of interest in going out as wanting to be only with her.

'He's very quiet,' Ellen's own mother had said.

'You know what they say about still waters, Mum,' Ellen had replied.

Liz knew intuitively that Alex's constant reference to his mother and her abandonment of him wasn't a good sign. His neediness wasn't a good sign. But she had ignored her misgivings, just as she had ignored so many other signs: the way he planned their evenings without asking her what she wanted to do; his obsessive need to always be on time; his dislike of her friends and parents—all rang alarm bells that Liz now knew she should have listened to. But if she ever expressed concern Alex would take her hand and kiss her palm and she would be sucked right back into the centre of his all-consuming love and she would dismiss the signs as bullshit.

She knew now that she should have seen all of the little things that had sometimes pricked at her as warning signs. She should have written them all down and it was possible that if she had read them on a list she would have walked away from him.

It was possible.

But back then she had fuck all idea of how to interpret those signs. She didn't want to read anything into them anyway. They could have been pasted on his head and she still would have missed them.

The signs were obscured by jazz evenings and too much red wine and oh, such fucking amazing sex. They were blurred by his charm and his smile and the way he waited for her at lunch, by the care he gave and attention he paid and the way he looked at her.

•

'He was the first man who bought me flowers,' said Glenda.

'He punched out some guy at work who was bothering me,' said Rhonda.

'He told me I was the most beautiful girl in the world,' said Cherry.

'He needed me,' said Liz.

•

'So do you want to go out or something?' asked Ellen, bringing Liz back to the present.

Liz nodded. A few free hours were a bit of a bonus and she knew she should use them. She could get her hair done or call a friend and go for coffee or even shop for some new clothes, but all of that felt like too much work—and it wasn't like she had money to throw away. Alex was being difficult about money.

•

'It's all about fucking control,' said Cherry. 'If I ask him for ten dollars the wanker gives me five so I always ask for double what I really need. If I don't ask him for money he gets the kids to ask me for something I can't afford so I have to ask him for the cash. Now that he can't hit me he needs to keep me under his thumb any way he can. He beat the crap out of some poor bloke who took me for a drink.' Cherry was only nineteen and the baby of the group but she was already saddled with two-year-old twin girls and enough cynicism to last her whole life.

Her boyfriend entered the loving phase whenever he was high and sucked Cherry back into his dreams of conquering the music world. But when the money ran out and he had no access to the drug he needed he came looking for Cherry to blame.

'I'd prefer him to smack the kids,' Cherry said, ignoring Rebecca's horrified face. 'It's about survival, isn't it?' Cherry's bitterness aged her twenty years and she made Liz feel naive.

'Did you tell the police your ex-boyfriend had assaulted the man who took you for a drink?' asked Rebecca, and they'd all had a good laugh at that.

•

Alex and Liz had only been separated for a few months and there was no way he was agreeing to mediation to work out the details of a divorce settlement until the twelve months were up. She would just have to hang on and hope that he gave her enough money to cover everything. Her father had sent her some cash when he heard that she had left Alex, but Luke needed things and groceries cost a lot. Alex put money into her account at the beginning of every month but Liz had noticed that each month it was dropping by a few hundred dollars. She didn't mention it. He asked her frequently if she had enough money, irritated by Liz's silence on the matter, but money was an argument that she couldn't even think how to start. She needed a lawyer and a proper agreement but she found herself so overwhelmed by the swirl of things she needed to do that she was usually still on the couch by the time Luke needed to be fetched from preschool.

'You need something to do,' said her mother, and then Liz did nothing just because there was a pissed-off twelve-year-old somewhere inside her still.

Liz needed a job but she would have to wait until Luke was at preschool full time. It was impossible for her to picture a future in which she lived alone and supported herself and her child. She felt the apathy of limbo pushing her back onto the couch every day.

Her mother didn't nag but Liz could sense her getting edgy as the weeks went by. They got on better now than they ever had but there would always be the leftover tension from Liz's teenage years, when her very presence and her likeness to her father were enough to depress her mother.

'You're welcome to go and live with your father and his cheap bit of fluff,' Ellen would say after arguments about everything from curfew to unloading the dishwasher.

The words had stung because Liz knew better than her mother that she was only tolerated in her father's house as a visitor. A closer relationship was never suggested. At fifteen Liz hated herself for all the same reasons the other girls did but she was always acutely aware that her parents no longer felt compelled to love her either.

She stood up straight and pretended she didn't care. Now that she had Luke she couldn't understand her parents' ambivalence to their own child, but as the years went on she could see a time when her own needs would challenge Luke's needs. What would it be like to be a single mother to a teenage boy?

Her mother hadn't mentioned rent—not yet. Liz was going to have to go to her father when she did. He wouldn't mind. He had always been generous with her. Giving her money meant he didn't have to get too involved in her life.

•

Ellen was still waiting for an answer.

'Why don't we just go out for coffee?' Liz said.

Ellen nodded and went to get her bag. She could have used a little time alone but Liz seemed to be in need of company.

It wasn't that she minded spending time with her daughter, but she had reached a point in her life where the silence of the house was a blessing. She adored Luke but his sounds and smells and bits and pieces somehow managed to migrate from his bedroom to every other part of the house.

Ellen needed time to recover her equilibrium. After a day playing with Luke and trying to tell Liz what she wanted to hear she needed some space to breathe. She had taken to staying up late at night waiting for Liz and Luke to fall asleep so that she could breathe in the silence.

It had taken years after Jack left to get used to being in the house at night when the noises began and every creak was a threat.

It had been years before she could sit in a restaurant alone or go to a movie or even take a walk without thinking that everyone who saw her knew she'd been left for a better woman. And now, when she was finally used to it, Luke and Liz had turned up and she couldn't turn them away. Whatever had happened between you, you didn't turn family away.

Liz understood how she felt about Alex anyway. She didn't need to say 'I told you so' because Liz knew what she was thinking. Somehow, in Liz's eyes, that made her a bad mother. What else was a mother for? If your mother couldn't tell you the truth, then who could? Liz threw words at her like 'supportive' and 'encouraging' but surely that was for children. She had been supported and encouraged when she learned to walk and talk and read and write. An adult needed to be told the truth. Wasn't the idea that her daughter didn't make the same mistakes she did? And yet here was Liz, back home after a messed-up marriage.

'I don't want to talk about it,' Liz had said.

Ellen wanted to talk about it. She wanted to say, 'What happened to the Liz I raised?'

But Liz had stopped talking to her after Jack left. At first Ellen hadn't cared. She lost interest in raising Liz as she nursed her own deep wounds. But her husband's decision wasn't all her fault. She was sure of that. Liz looked at her like she had failed.

Ellen could trace Liz's disdain back to the very day Jack left. She knew she had behaved badly. The shame of it coloured her cheeks even now, all these years later, but she had been afraid. She had not known how she would survive in the world without Jack and so she had pulled at his clothes and begged and cried until he had driven away in his truck.

It wasn't that she was so in love with him by then. If anything there had been times when she could not fathom how she could bear to spend the rest of her life with him, but he made the choice for both of them. He took control and she couldn't seem to think straight.

She couldn't forget the way Liz had looked at her that day. There had been no sympathy from her twelve-year-old daughter, only judgement and disgust.

Liz retreated into herself then. She was silent on the things that mattered in her life and Ellen knew she had never pushed too hard for communication. She had been busy drowning her sorrows and trying to figure out where her life had gone wrong.

Ellen watched Liz put up walls when she began dating, watched her protect herself, and she was pleased. She wanted better for her daughter. She wanted Liz to have the control. But then Alex had come along. Liz had seemed to have the upper hand until Luke was born. Motherhood turned Liz into a simpering creature, afraid of using the wrong words. Ellen imagined that it was post-natal depression, but then Liz turned up on her doorstep; in the clichéd dark glasses.

She wanted to shake her daughter and ask her what she had been thinking when she let a man hit her.

No one had ever been allowed to hit Liz.

When she was about two Ellen had lashed out as Liz threw her food on the floor for the third time and Jack had stood towering above her, shaking with rage. 'You don't hit a child, Ellen,' he said. 'You don't ever hit my child.'

It had been an extreme reaction and Ellen understood, not for the first time, that her giant of a husband held some secrets that would never be told.

Jack's parents were both in a nursing home in Perth, paid for by Jack and visited by his sister who occasionally phoned with updates.

Once they realised that there would be no more children Ellen and Jack spent their remaining married years worshipping at the altar of their perfect Elizabeth. When Ellen thought back in her more lucid moments she would realise that Liz was probably the only thing that kept them together beyond the first years of their marriage.

After Jack left Ellen couldn't help comparing the two of them as they both took up her space and towered over her. And then Liz's childhood was over and she was married to Alex and Ellen was completely alone for the first time in decades and she was surprised to find that she liked it.

Now Liz was home again. And when Ellen caught sight of her

changing one day she could see that the bruises fading to yellow spoke of a longer story than just one black eye.

She wanted to tell Jack, but Liz begged her not to. Nevertheless, she had called him one night when Liz was asleep.

'I just wanted to tell you,' she had begun and then she had heard another voice enter the room. 'Honey,' it had whined seductively and Ellen hadn't been able to make the words come out. She just put down the phone then. Jack didn't call her back to ask what was wrong. She wasn't his problem anymore.

•

They drove to the nearby shopping centre and parked, writing down the colour and number of their row. Ellen had once been lost in the car park for close to an hour when the shopping centre first opened. Liz preferred hanging out in the library to shopping. Luke would climb in and out of the old boat filled with stuffed toys and she would leaf through old magazines and imagine a different life for herself.

Walking past a shop Liz caught sight of the two of them reflected in the window and almost laughed aloud at the odd picture they made.

Ellen wore her hair in a neat bob and tucked starched shirts into capri pants and her feet into dainty ballet flats. Liz always had bits of hair escaping and her shirt hanging out. Even though Luke was three already she had never quite managed to lose the baby weight. He mother made her feel the same way she had when she was twelve and towered over all the petite, flat-chested girls at school—out of place.

Her height couldn't be disguised by stooping so eventually she just stood up straight, towering over her small, neat mother and just about everyone else she knew. She felt awkward standing next to her mother, she felt self-conscious standing next to her friends and she was generally ill at ease whenever someone looked up at her. Alex didn't think she took up too much space. At first.

•

They wandered aimlessly in and out of stores filled with the colours of autumn. The chill in the open-air mall forced them into a coffee shop where they ordered tea. 'I think I'll have a slice of the mud cake as well,' said Liz and Ellen had to bite her lip to keep quiet. Her daughter spilled out of the chair. Where once she had been statuesque, she was now just big. Ellen couldn't see Liz being able to pull herself together and get on with things.

'You know there are a lot of people finding themselves new partners on the internet these days,' said Ellen.

'I've only been separated a few months, Mum, stop trying to marry me off again. And by the way, you're not exactly the best example. You haven't made any effort to find someone else.'

'It's a bit late for me now, but it's not too late for you, Liz. There's nothing wrong with a few dates.'

Liz only had eyes for Luke and Ellen could see the hold Alex still had over her. When he came over to get Luke Liz would watch him and her eyes would glaze a little. Ellen didn't understand what her daughter saw in him. He had nice hair and nice eyes but otherwise there was nothing remarkable about him. He was just shy of skinny and he had small hands. Ellen hated the idea of small hands on a man. But of course they were big enough to do some damage. They were big enough for that.

Jack had never liked him either. 'He has soft hands,' he told Ellen when they were planning the wedding.

'He's an engineer, Jack,' said Ellen. She kept her reservations to herself around her ex-husband. Disagreeing with him was more important. 'Not everyone has to be a piano mover.'

Jack had not taken the bait. 'I know what he does,' he said. 'But his hands are soft and he's shorter than she is.'

Ellen had just shrugged, and only remembered defending Alex when Liz had turned up on her doorstep.

Liz's mobile rang and from the way she answered it Ellen knew it was Alex. He couldn't even deal with his son for a few hours without calling Liz. Ellen couldn't see how they would ever be free of him. Liz refused to get the police involved.

'Luke needs his father,' she said. And that was that.

•

'Hi, babe, I just wanted to tell you that he's fine and having fun,' said Alex. He was back in charming mode as if that morning's conversation had never happened.

'Great,' said Liz. She wasn't sure of the real reason for the call. She knew that he couldn't simply have called to tell her Luke was okay. There was always a reason. Alex was planning to wear her down. He was starting by calling her 'babe' and would keep going from there.

•

'They call you babe *and* sweetie *and* my love *and for some reason you think that no one will ever love you like this man does,' said Rhonda. 'No one will ever think you're as beautiful as he does and you get sucked back in and then, when your ribs are so bruised you can't breathe, you remember that no one will ever hurt you like this man does either. And you think that you'll never get sucked in again and then he calls you up and calls you* babe *and you're fucked.'*

•

Liz knew that the manipulation was supposed to end when she packed her suitcase and walked out the door. It was supposed to be the full stop at the end of her very long sentence. She was

supposed to be free to start a new chapter. But the way he said 'babe' dragged her back every time. The conversations she had with him in her head were no defence against his actual presence.

She'd thought she had worked out a way to listen to him without letting him change her thinking. She'd thought the time apart had made her impervious to his subtle machinations. She was wrong.

She took a deep breath and steeled herself to end the call quickly.

'Thanks for the call, Alex. He needs to be home by two and don't forget to take him to the bathroom.'

'I know how to take care of my child, Liz. You don't need to tell me what to do with him every fucking minute.'

Liz rubbed her forehead in the overheated coffee shop. She had messed up again. 'Sorry, Alex, I'm sorry. Of course you know how to take care of him. I'll see you later. Have a good time, okay?'

'Don't you want to speak to your son, Liz?'

'No, it's okay. Let him play. I'll see you guys later.'

'But don't you want to tell him you love him?'

'I have to go now, Alex, I need . . . I need to drive.'

She hung up the phone and wiped her sweaty palm on the tablecloth. It always felt like she was just one wrong sentence away from him going off the deep end. Why the insistence that she tell Luke she loved him? That was a new twist.

Liz took a sip of her tea and waited for her heart to slow. Who knew why Alex did anything? Right now she just wanted five minutes off from thinking about him.

•

Ellen stirred her tea, trying to figure out how to ask the question that had been playing on her mind for weeks. Liz had never said anything about the way Alex treated Luke. She seemed happy enough to let Luke go with him but Ellen couldn't help worrying when she saw Liz planning each sentence, desperate not to upset the man.

'You don't think he'd ever hit Luke, do you?' she said. The words leapt out into the air without waiting for a better time.

'Mum, don't be ridiculous. Come on, let's just go home. I can grab forty winks before they get back. I promised Luke pizza tonight.'

Ellen sighed and paid the bill. They drove home in silence. Ellen had already suggested the police and a lawyer. She supposed she should be grateful that Liz went to a support group, although she didn't know what help the other women could be. They were all in the same boat and so far none of them seemed to have found a way off onto land.

At home they went their separate ways. Ellen made herself another cup of tea and added a dash of whisky. 'Just to get me through the day,' she told herself.

•

Liz went up to her bedroom and lay on her bed. She had managed an hour or two of regret-filled sleep before Luke had climbed into bed with her and snuggled up to watch the sun rise.

Liz didn't mind the early mornings. Luke would mumble things and sing to himself and stroke her hair. It was really the only time she could give him a proper cuddle. During the day he was always getting on with the serious business of exploring his world. He wanted to feed himself and dress himself and he wouldn't let her kiss him anymore.

She closed her eyes and tried to wash away the image of herself and Alex on the kitchen floor. Last night he'd used the word 'beautiful' as he touched her, but only a few months ago she had been 'a fat cow' and 'as big as a bus'. She was also 'stupid as fuck' and 'completely naive'.

When she repeated the phrases back to him he denied ever having said them, and when she showed him a bruise he asked her how it had happened.

•

'They block it out,' said Glenda. 'After they've put their fist through a wall or into your face they just block it out. They say sorry but they don't really know what for. That's why they can't understand what you're so upset with them about.' Glenda's husband was a respected member of the community and someone others turned to for advice and help. But it seemed that Glenda wasn't respectful enough. She seemed unaware of his status as a leader of the community and that bothered him. It bothered him a great deal.

'Bullshit,' said Rhonda. 'They know what they've done. They

just don't want to fucking acknowledge it. Dr Phil says you can't change what you don't acknowledge.'

'Oh, fuck, Rhonda,' said Cherry, whose parents wanted a daughter who was sweet and kind instead of the messed-up teenager with an abusive drug-addicted boyfriend they got. 'You watch too much television.'

•

Liz turned on her side and felt herself drifting towards sleep. The words hung around longer than the bruises. They jumped out at her when she looked in a mirror or tried on an old skirt. A bruise changed colour and faded away and in time it was possible to look at the place where she had been marked and not really be able to see anything at all. But what he said and the way he said it was in the air. It became part of what she breathed. His disgust ate away at her insides and however much she tried to smother it with sugar and salt it was always there. It was always just another reason why she deserved what she got.

Her body relaxed completely.

Luke would be home soon and they would have pizza.

He would be home soon and they would have pizza and he would tell her exactly how many times he had been down the slide.

Right now that would have to be enough.

4

In the park Alex watched Luke go up the ladder and down the slide ten times.

'Watch me, Dad, watch me now, okay? Watch how I go down. See how fast I went? Watch me again, okay?'

Alex smiled and waved every time Luke got to the top of the ladder. Luke wouldn't go down the slide without the wave.

The park was full of fathers and their kids.

They all had 'Saturday access visit' floating above their heads. Everyone was too happy. Everyone was trying too fucking hard. No one said no to an ice cream or an extra ride on the swings or another round of junk food. A whole week needed to be lived in this single day. Luke forgot his days as soon as they ended. Alex had to push and lead him to a memory, hoping to get something he could hold on to for the next few days.

'What did you learn in preschool this week, Luke?'

'What did you eat for dinner last night?'

'Who did you play with at preschool?'

'I don't know, Dad,' Luke would say. 'I forgetted already.'

Under a tree there was a father with teenage children and Alex could see the guy had really made an effort. He had a picnic basket and a special mat and a collection of board games. His teenage sons had not even looked up from their mobile phones yet. Kids could be such arseholes.

Now Luke wanted his dad to watch everything he did, but Alex could see that it was inevitable they would end up like the family under the tree. If you lived apart it got harder and harder to keep in touch. Kids didn't want to repeat the same story about what happened at school that day twice. Relationships were held together by the words thrown casually over a shoulder on the way to school or to a movie. Serious conversations took place in the car or just before bedtime. You couldn't schedule a kid's interest in sharing something with you. You just couldn't.

With each passing week it became clearer to him that it would be impossible to hold on to his boy as he grew up and pushed at the boundaries that made him feel so safe now. Right now Luke thought Alex was a superhero and that's how a boy should think of his father. If he wasn't with Luke all the time there would be no way he could be sure of his love. Eventually he and Luke would just stop talking.

Alex felt a quick stab in his chest. A premonition of the pain to come.

He remembered being in the park with Liz and Luke when Luke was about a year old and spotting the sad little groups and feeling just a little smug that he wasn't them. He had seen other fathers looking over at his little family with envy and he thought, 'That's right—you should envy me. I have it all.'

And now here he was, just another Saturday dad.

Luke went up the slide and down the slide and Alex took a moment to hate Liz. He wanted to push his fist through her face. The rage came in waves now and there was nowhere for it to wash up so it never dissipated. At home, at the house where his family used to live, he broke things and threw things and punched the wall but nothing helped. He always had to repair everything afterwards. He didn't want Liz to come home and see the damage. He kept the house nice for her.

He hated the way she had looked at him when he picked up Luke. She was so calm, so calculating. She twisted his words and told him what he felt.

When they had been together she had been careful not to do that.

This whole separation thing had been totally her idea and hers alone, yet she wanted him to agree that they were better apart. She wanted him to embrace the concept like the end of his family didn't make him want to . . . to . . . He rubbed his hands through his hair, trying to rub away the ugly thoughts, but he could feel the rage simmering.

Last night she had used him. She had played with him, luring him in with wine and dinner and then she had just stood there, inviting him to touch her. Now she wanted him to crawl back into his box and behave. How could she think she could get away with treating him like that?

She thought she was holding all the cards. That was the problem. She thought she could just walk away and leave him and somehow make it his fault. He wasn't buying it, not any of it.

Liz knew that most of their problems had nothing to do with him. She had known who he was when they got married. She had loved him then; even though he could sense she was holding herself back a little, he knew she loved him. He needed to get through to her, he wanted to smash down the walls that she surrounded herself with. He was always aware that he loved her just a little more than she loved him.

That was probably something that mother of hers had taught her. Ellen was always going on about what a bastard Liz's father was. No one could hate a man like his ex-wife could and that was the truth.

Things had changed after Luke arrived. Liz had acted like she was the only woman who had ever had a baby. She hadn't exactly been an earth mother. She hated being sleep-deprived and having to be at home all the time with the baby but that was what a mother did. It was the first time he could feel that she needed him more than he needed her. He liked the way that felt.

Sometimes he had hated her then as well. She was always leaking milk or crying about no sleep. She wanted him to help with the baby all the time but he had to go to work. He had loved her more, too. The desperation in her voice when she called him at work was like a balm. He had been the best husband he could be. He had bought her flowers and cooked her favourite food and he had always found her so sexy, so beautiful.

But those months had passed and Liz had become her old self again.

She didn't ask for things or beg him to stay home. She just demanded. Sometimes her voice made his skin itch.

Sometimes he had done things he wasn't proud of, but Liz wouldn't listen to reason. He hadn't asked much of her. Every man wanted a clean house and a well-behaved child. Cooking your husband a meal when he came home from work wasn't too much to ask, was it?

It irritated him when she didn't want to be perfect for him after Luke was born. She would say, 'I'm so fat,' and he would disagree and tell her how beautiful she was but then he would see her eat a whole bag of chips and he would be disgusted with her.

He took care of himself so she would always find him attractive. It should have been important to her to look the way he wanted her to look.

He tried to control his anger around her but she liked to see him angry. Maybe it turned her on? She would goad him into doing something she didn't like and then she would cry and sulk and refuse to see that he was really sorry.

Women were all alike that way.

His mother had walked away and left him and his father and she had never even bothered to explain why. Frank would have apologised for whatever he had done to piss her off, if she had just given him a chance. But women didn't like apologies. Saying sorry wasn't enough for them.

'There's no forgiveness in a woman's heart, son, remember that,' his father had said. He had picked Alex up from school and told him in a flat voice that his mother was gone. 'Like on a holiday?' Alex had asked.

'No, son, she won't be back.'

Alex hadn't understood. Every day he had asked when his mother would be home and every day his father had told him never.

'How long is never?' Alex had asked.

'Never is like until you're dead,' said his father.

It had been a difficult thing for a five-year-old to understand, but eventually Alex had.

He had asked why and where she had gone but his father was done with explanations. His father wasn't a bad man, he was just heartbroken. Alex could see that now. He could feel that now.

He liked going over to visit Frank these days. In his father's study Liz and all her bullshit were crowded out with beer and sports and vacant blonde girls in bikinis.

His father had learned to stay away from love.

He had Barbara now, but she wasn't an essential part of his life.

Barbara knocked on the study door and was invited in to deliver snacks. His father never thanked her and she didn't seem to need to be acknowledged. It was easy just forgetting for a few hours. The anger dissolved in the cold beer and he always felt better afterwards.

Barbara sometimes called him 'son' but it was just a word to her. At five he would have attached himself to anyone who came into his life and tried to mother him but now he just looked at Barbara the same way his father did. If she fucked off tomorrow neither man would care.

As a kid he had wanted to talk about his mother, he wanted to keep who she was fresh in his head, but even mentioning her was forbidden. It only took one backhander from his father for him to learn that lesson.

Sometimes he would hide in a cupboard and whisper, 'Hi, Mum. I had a fun day at school today. Mum, can you make me a sandwich with peanut butter? Do you want to see the picture I drew at school today, Mum? Please, Mum. I love you, Mum.'

He was the only person in his class without a mother. He missed seeing her at school when it was time for a concert or an art show. His father came to everything. Alex would seek him out in the audience to find him looking at his feet, uncomfortable surrounded by women.

He watched the other mothers smiling up at their children, snapping photographs and readying words of praise, and he felt an ache that he preferred to dismiss as hunger.

He told the other kids in the class that his mother lived overseas with a prince and then he got into trouble for lying. He got into trouble a lot for lying, but people preferred the lies. His father wanted to know that he was top of the class and girls wanted to know that he was rich. The teachers loved to hear his sad stories and his friends liked to think he and his father did nothing but party. People preferred the lies, so that's what he gave them and then they stretched their mouths in horror and shook their heads when the lies fell apart.

He missed the way his mother used to cook. His father had to learn to cook and he had never really mastered the art.

Alex told him he was really happy with his meals, though. Alex told his father he was just fine and even if he tried to tell him something else, all his father heard was that he was fine.

The other thing he missed was being touched. When he went over to friends' houses he would feel sick with envy watching the casual way other mothers touched their sons. They rubbed their backs and stroked their arms or ruffled their hair as they walked past. They were just casual touches and Alex hadn't even realised that he was experiencing them until they were gone. Sometimes he would sit right up next to his father just to feel the touch of the skin on his arm. 'Jesus, Alex, there's a whole sofa. Move up.'

Luke liked a cuddle. Alex felt like he could hold him forever. Sometimes he would squeeze him a little too tight and Luke would giggle, 'No, Daddy, stop, Daddy.'

He missed being able to lie next to Luke as he fell asleep.

'Watch me, Daddy, watch me again.'

'I'm watching. One, two, three, go!'

When he was eighteen he had gone looking for his mother. The internet made everything easy. One day Alex just typed his mother's maiden name into the telephone directory and there she was. She was living in Queensland and she even had a Facebook page. He couldn't believe it. A fucking Facebook page. She was right out in the open just waiting to be found.

There was only one picture he could see but it looked like she'd moved right along from her first husband and son. She had a new man and two daughters to keep her company. She was laughing in the picture and she looked so different to the woman he remembered that he questioned whether it was really her, but it was. He just knew it was. Her smile taunted him and he knew he would never try to contact her. He wondered what she would say if he requested to be her friend on Facebook. He wondered if she would be horrified or happy. Would she rush over to where he was and embrace him? Would she get down on her knees and beg his forgiveness? Alex studied the picture and then he closed the page.

In her face there was no evidence of his existence.

It had made him so angry, so completely full of rage, that he'd had to get out of the house and just run until there was nothing left.

How could a woman just leave her child? How could she just leave and pretend he had never existed?

Every year he promised himself that he would contact her and ask why, but he never did. He was afraid of the answer.

As a five-year-old he had known that it was him his mother was leaving. His room was always messy and sometimes he whined when she asked him to do something. He didn't like to have a bath and he never wanted to go to bed when it was time.

As an adult he understood that her leaving had nothing to do with him. But she should have loved him enough to stay and take care of him. However bad it had been with his father, she should have loved him enough.

His mother was the person at fault. She was an evil woman

who didn't know how to love. He would never get in contact with her because she didn't deserve to have a son like him.

He wanted to share his discovery with his father but he knew the rules when it came to his mother. Even at eighteen he knew it was better to stick to the rules.

His father seemed happy enough with Barbara. They had been together for about five years now. She liked cigarettes and a glass of wine or two at night and so did his father. She cooked nice meals and his father only complained about her wanting him to do things in the house every few months.

Barbara didn't like Liz. She thought she was 'up herself'.

Alex was certain of Frank's love. His father had even uttered the words 'I love you' once or twice when Alex was growing up. But even as an adult some small part of Alex was surprised when he turned up to his father's house and the man was still there and still interested in seeing him.

Now here he was in the same position his dad had been. His wife had left him. But Liz had taken her child with her. Alex envied Luke that a little. He would have gone with his mother if she had asked him. He loved his dad but he was only a kid and he would have gone with his mother if she had asked.

Alex rubbed his face, trying to get rid of his anger. Liz was such a bitch—he couldn't believe he had ever fallen for her. He wished there was a way to make her sorry for hurting him. Women shouldn't be allowed to do this. They shouldn't be allowed to take your kid and then tell you when you could visit. She hadn't even wanted to talk to Luke when he called her. Why should she get to have the kid full time?

It was getting close to lunch time and even though Liz liked Luke to eat healthy foods, Alex would take him to some fast-food place instead. Nothing wrong with a bit of junk food every now and again.

Later he would call her again. He kept trying to let go but it felt like Liz had her hands tangled in his soul.

One minute he hated her so completely he thought he was free of her and the next minute he would remember the way her face looked when she saw Luke for the first time and he would love her again.

If she could just see his point of view, if she could just understand how important it was for them to be a family, it would all be okay again. He wasn't a bad guy; he was willing to forgive her if she said sorry and came back.

He always gave people another chance. His father believed that everyone only got to fuck up once, but Alex liked to give them another chance.

He had made some mistakes with Liz and he wasn't going to deny it, but he had apologised.

He would give Luke lunch and then he would call her again and maybe they could have a proper conversation without that mother of hers interfering.

Ellen was a big part of the problem in their marriage. Alex knew from day one that she didn't like him. The first time they had dinner together Ellen had asked about his family, and when he told her about his mother she had been like a dog with a bone. She just wouldn't let go, asking question after question.

When he told her that he and Liz wanted to start a family right away she had just laughed and told them that babies were forever and they should live a little first. Like they were fucking teenagers who didn't know what they wanted.

Alex had had to look down at his plate and just chew his rage away then. He couldn't exactly yell at Liz's mother, although he did think that it would have been better if the woman had not been in Liz's life at all. She was a bad influence. Alex could always tell when Liz had been talking to her mother. She got a little aggressive and tried to order him around. She needed to be set straight and then she would cry and threaten to leave him like it had been his fault.

Alex had tried to get Ellen to like him. He always bought her a nice bottle of whisky and he laughed at her stupid jokes. He complimented her hair and her clothes and told her she was sexy for an older woman, but Ellen just didn't want to like him. It wasn't his fault she was so screwed up about men.

He looked at his watch. It was nearly one already but that was okay. He was in no hurry to get Luke home. No hurry at all.

He would call Liz again later and give her another chance. That was just the kind of guy he was. Today would be the day that she agreed to come home. He could feel it. Last night they had been so happy together. Alex knew it could be like that all the time. He felt his true love for Liz erode his anger. Today she would be coming home. If he kept Luke with him a little longer she would have time to think about how important it was to be a family. She would have time to realise how much she needed him in her life.

'Come on, Luke,' he said. 'Lunch time.'

'Yay!' said Luke. 'Lunch time, yay!'

Twenty minutes late

'Good afternoon, West Wood police station, how can I help you?'

'Um, yeah, hi, um . . . look, I don't know if I should be calling you yet but my husband is late bringing my son back from his access visit—well, it's not formal or anything, I mean we haven't signed any papers. So it's not really an access visit, not yet . . . The thing is, he was supposed to be here by two and he's not.'

Constable Lisa Mitchell looked at her watch. 'What am I?' she thought. West Wood police station had more crackpot calls than anywhere else in the country. That's what it felt like, anyway. She'd sent a car over to a domestic dispute over who owned Aunty Thelma's necklace three times today because different neighbours kept calling and reporting a disturbance. One old man had called four times to report a lost parrot and there must have been some bored teenagers as well because some of the callers descended into giggles after they reported aliens landing on the roof and a gorilla in the back garden.

'You should try working in the Cross,' her friend Emma said. 'There every call is a bloody emergency.'

Lisa smarted at the comparison. It wasn't as if she hadn't wanted the Cross. You got your placement and you went where you were told to go. She should have stayed in Melbourne. At least there she'd seen some action.

'Your time will come,' Robert assured her.

'Yeah, but right now I'm stuck in the suburbs.'

'It's not so bad,' said Robert. 'I'm stuck in the suburbs as well and you never would have met me in the Cross.'

She sighed. Outright rudeness to the public was actively discouraged.

'He's only twenty minutes late, ma'am. Have you tried calling him?'

The woman on the other end of the phone was quiet for a moment and Lisa knew she thought it was a stupid question, but Lisa had been on the desk for six weeks now, long enough to learn that there were no stupid questions.

'Yes,' said the woman. 'Obviously I've tried calling him. He's not answering his phone.'

'Is there any reason why you are so concerned? Has your husband done anything to make you concerned for your child?'

'What? Oh no. I mean no, of course he hasn't. I just wondered if there had been an accident or something. I'm just . . . I'm just worried, you know?'

Lisa thought, 'Why don't I just search the computer for every car accident in the last twenty minutes and we can go through them? Or I could call around to every police station across the country and ask if anyone has seen a car accident.'

Aloud, she said, 'I completely understand, ma'am, but there isn't much we can do. Family law is dealt with by the federal police. If you have a formal agreement and he has to have the child back at a set time then we can get the federal police to look into the matter.'

Lisa didn't say that there was little chance the federal police would get involved unless they thought the kid was in danger, and for them to do anything at all they needed a recovery order. The whole process could take weeks.

'But I don't have any agreements in place. We haven't been separated for very long.'

'Then I'm afraid he is actually doing nothing wrong. He is not required to have the child back at any time.'

'Well he agreed to have him back by two. I told him to have him home by two.'

'I understand, but custody is fifty/fifty until there have been agreements made in court. So as I said there is really nothing we can do. He can keep the child past the agreed time if he chooses to do so.'

'But that's not right! He told me he would have him home by two.'

'I'm sorry, ma'am. There is nothing we can do at present.'

'Nothing . . . are you sure can't you put out a . . . what do you call it? You know, ask them to look for him?'

The whole world thought the American cop shows were real life.

'You could come in and make a missing persons report but I can't simply tell the police to look for someone because he's twenty minutes late.'

'Don't I have to wait twenty-four hours to do that?'

'No, ma'am. If you have some concern for the welfare of the missing person you can make a report as early as you want. Are you concerned for your child's welfare?'

'He's not really missing. I mean, I don't really know where he is but he is with his father. I'm just worried about him.'

'I understand, but we cannot do anything. It's not illegal to be late.'

'Oh . . . oh, I'm sorry, of course you can't. I just . . .'

'Ma'am, is there a reason you are concerned for your son?' The woman on the other end of the phone sounded like she was getting teary. It was an extreme reaction to someone being a few minutes late. Lisa felt a small shiver run down her spine.

'No . . . I guess not . . . It's just that we had a fight and I'm, you know, I'm worried.'

Lisa could hear a whole other story behind the word 'fight' but it wasn't possible to demand the truth from the woman. That only happened after things went pear-shaped, after the dad took the kid and . . . shit, now she remembered why she had left Melbourne. As if she ever needed reminding.

'Look,' said Lisa, knowing that she should just hang up the phone, knowing that the police weren't there to chase up everyone who was a few minutes late, knowing that the woman was probably just an ex with a grudge. 'Look,' she said, because she knew how horrible it was to feel powerless and part of the reason she became a police officer was so that no one would ever make her feel powerless again, 'maybe you can give me his number plate and I'll keep an eye out for any accident reports. He's probably just stuck in traffic. You know how traffic can be.'

'Yeah, and his mobile is probably just out of battery. He never remembers to charge it.' The woman laughed, comforted by these reasonable explanations.

'I'm sure that's it,' agreed Lisa, conscious of the other lines lighting up. 'You can come in and talk to one of the other constables, if you'd like.'

'No . . . no, I can't leave. He could be back any moment and then Luke might be a bit upset if I wasn't here. So I can just give you his number plate and you can kind of keep a lookout?'

'Okay,' said Lisa. She would take down the number to make the woman feel better, but realistically there was not much she could do.

'Um, his number plate is WVX 216—no, 217. Yeah, that's it: WVX 217.'

'Are you certain that's correct?'

'Yes, I'm sure. It's a blue car—a Toyota sedan. It's five years old.'

'And can I have his name, your name and your son's name?'

The woman on the phone spelled the names out slowly.

People liked to give you their details. They felt something was happening when they had to spell out their names slowly and clearly. At the end of each shift Lisa usually had a pile of names for the recycling bin. People hardly ever called back. Sometimes they just needed someone to talk to.

'Okay, ma'am, we'll look into it. Let us know when he comes in.'

'Yes, thanks, I will.'

Lisa disconnectd and answered the next call. The woman wouldn't call back. The ex and the kid would be home soon and the woman would be too busy with other stuff to remember she had called the station.

Every day there were calls like this. Husbands who came home late and kids who ignored their curfews. If they followed up on all of them they would never get any real policing done.

But there was something in the woman's voice. Who got concerned when their ex was only twenty minutes late? As far as Lisa could tell, bringing the kid back late was standard procedure for divorcing parents. Bringing the kid back late was just another tactic in the guerrilla warfare of divorce.

After Lisa had told an old woman locked out of her house to go next door and call a locksmith and taken down the name of a missing cat, she looked at the number plate again. Something about it made her heart beat just a little faster.

'It's probably nothing,' she told herself. 'You're just bored.'

She stared at the number plate for a few more minutes and then went over to the computer. She could look it up. It would pass some time.

Last year a mother had called in to say her husband was late coming back from a visit and by the time she filed the report and a recovery order had been issued, the guy had already left the country with their three kids. As far as Lisa knew, the feds were still looking for them.

The internet was full of stories of kids who never came back from their access visits. All over television and the movies people were always bleating about the needs of the kids when there was a divorce but no matter how much information was around, no matter how educated the parents were, there would always be those who stopped seeing their children and started seeing little negotiation hostages. People forgot themselves in a divorce. They were hurt and angry and mourning the loss of the lives they were supposed to have had, and if they could use the kids to get back at the ex that was just fine.

Lately, though, things seemed to be getting worse. There was that father who just drove his car into a lake and watched his three kids drown. He just got out of the car and swam away and watched the car sink. He didn't even call the police or emergency services. He went straight to the ex-wife to tell her what he'd done. Of course he claimed it was an accident. His wife believed it had been an accident at first. She didn't understand that he could hate her enough to hurt his own kids.

People lost their ability to feel anything but their own pain and sometimes they spread it around. Mostly it was the men who hurt their kids. That was just the way it was. You could argue all you liked that women did as much damage as men, but the facts were the facts. Women couldn't kill their kids just to get back at their ex; that would be like killing themselves.

She looked at the number plate again. Then the phone rang.

'Good afternoon, West Wood police station, how can I help you?'

5

Liz put down the phone. She was just being silly, she really was. The woman at the police station must have thought she was a complete lunatic.

She dialled Alex's number again and left another message. 'Hi, Alex, it's me again. I just wanted to know where the two of you were. I hope you're having fun. I may have forgotten to tell you that I wanted to put Luke down for a nap at two today. So if you guys could come home that would be great. Call me when you get this message. Thanks.'

She made sure not to nag or accuse or criticise. She kept her voice warm and friendly. When she put the phone down she felt a small stab of hate for the woman she became when she spoke to Alex. She was fucking pathetic. So cautious, so placating.

It reminded her a little of the way her mother sounded the first year after she and Liz's father divorced. Ellen would call Jack and ask silly questions she already knew the answer to and she would make jokes and tell him that only he knew how to do certain things in the house. Liz had needed to leave the room during those calls.

Now here she was, working to keep her soon-to-be-ex-husband on side.

Sometimes you were so busy looking back at the person you didn't want to become that you tripped right into someone you had never imagined you could be.

He wasn't going to come over and hit her. That was the theory anyway. She had removed herself from the situation and she was out of his reach but her body was having a hard time catching up with what she knew in her mind. Her body reacted with a racing heart and wet palms every time she heard his voice drop a note or saw his eyes darken.

Living in his house, the voice she used with him had been about survival, but now she wanted to grab herself by the shoulders and shake until she grew some balls.

At university it had been a standing joke that Liz Searle would dominate all tutorial discussions.

'You just take over and don't give anyone else a chance to talk,' her best friend Molly had laughed.

'I have a lot of opinions,' said Liz.

'You definitely are not short of opinions. You stomp all over everybody else's ideas. Men don't like women who don't shut up.'

'God, Molly, you don't shut up either. Besides, who really cares what men think?'

And then she had met Alex and she had just disappeared.

Molly hadn't understood the attraction. She had been especially negative about Alex's neediness.

'Christ, Liz,' Molly had said. 'They all need us. It's like the oldest fucking trick in the book.'

'It doesn't feel like a trick,' said Liz.

'Of course it is. You're being manipulated into loving him. Is that what you really want? Some guy who's looking for another mummy? Give it a few more weeks and you'll be doing his washing and making him soup when he's sick.'

'He's not looking for another mother. His mother left when he was five years old. He was raised by his dad. And is it so bad if I do some washing for him or make him soup or take care of him? Isn't that what love is about? People in love take care of each other.'

Even as the words floated into the air Liz had realised that she knew very little about love. She had drifted through high school mostly ignored or taunted, and first-year university had only brought men looking for conquests. At home she had only lived with the dissolution of love. The gradual fading away of something she had not been around to witness at the beginning and so could not even remember having existed.

'Did he tell you that?' said Molly, laughing. 'Those words sound like they come straight from his mouth.'

'What if he did? Why are you so against this guy?'

'I'm not against him, Liz. I'm against who you are when you're with him. You're getting all soppy and sentimental. Washing a guy's undies doesn't get any better just because you're in love. You're still washing his underwear.'

'Stop being gross, Molly. I really like him, okay? There's something different about him. He's had a hard life. How would you like to have grown up without a mother?'

'Oh God,' said Molly. 'This is not a good sign. Now you'll have to be his mummy. Dump him while you still can and let me introduce you to the guy in my physics class.'

There was a moment when Liz thought that Molly had a point, but it was only a moment. Molly had always told her the truth ever since the day they met, standing in line to register for classes. Liz had been busy taking in the other students, watching cute boys and embracing the smell of freedom, when she stepped forward into Molly and dropped everything she was carrying. 'Well that's just embarrassing,' said the girl with curly brown hair and green eyes. Liz had looked up with a scowl on her face to find the girl smiling at her. She laughed with relief, 'Yeah, it is.'

To Liz, her very existence was a constant source of discomfiture. She stood too high above the crowd. She looked down on too many young men. Now she looked down on the girl poured into skinny jeans and felt the relief of not being judged just yet.

'It's a good thing you bumped into me. I'm Molly Lavender Bright. Please don't ask me about my name—my parents are leftover hippies and I'm going to change it by deed poll any minute now. I feel like I've been here all day. I'm thirsty, are you thirsty? I can show you the best coffee shop on campus.'

They had gone for coffee and discovered they were both going to be primary school teachers. Molly was completely certain of her place in the world so Liz was happy to defer to her opinion in social matters just as Molly was happy to trust Liz's ideas in class. Molly had spent high school flirting and dating and breaking hearts. Liz was glad to be pulled from her books and into the social whirl that was Molly. There were parties and dinners and nightclubs, and Liz managed to lose her stubborn virgin status and see it only as a step towards finding the right man.

Molly copied Liz's notes and they both waxed lyrical over small children and minds that could be shaped.

Liz left the remembered terrors of high school behind and shared her dreams with her new friend. She felt herself to be a completely different person, no longer hemmed in by the things she heard at school or the words her mother threw at her. It was late to tread the path of self-discovery, but Liz had spent her teenage years dealing with her mother and the bottle by her mother's side.

Only Alex divided them. Molly kept telling Liz to let go and move on.

'Sometimes he's a little bit creepy,' said Molly. 'He has this weird way of looking at you, like he's obsessed. I bet he's covered his whole bedroom in pictures of you so he can watch you all night.'

'Rubbish, Molly, you're just making that up,' said Liz.

She liked the way Alex looked at her and she hoped he did have pictures of her in his room. She carried a picture of him in her wallet.

She liked that he was completely in love whereas she was holding a little back. Just a small piece of herself was being kept safe in case. In case it all went wrong. Liz didn't mention this to Molly. It was too weird a concept to share with the world.

'If you love him so much, take a little time away, get some perspective. Come with me to London for a few months. Your dad would spring for a ticket and we'll have the best time.'

A trip to London was right at the top of Liz's wish list. But she couldn't take time away and she couldn't let go because he needed her. He needed her more than anyone had ever needed her. She couldn't explain to Molly what it felt like to have someone who checked in with you every day, who cared what you thought and who claimed to only be functioning in class because of you.

Liz knew what it was like for a woman not to be needed or even wanted by a man, and she couldn't explain that to Molly. Molly wouldn't understand because she came from a family that was still glued together.

Mum and dad and two brothers and Molly, all living together in one big happy house. Molly was needed by everyone in her family. Her mother needed her to babysit her brothers and her father needed her to help him with the computer and her brothers needed her to play with them and the whole family needed her to be home at dinner so they could discuss how everybody's day had gone.

Alex was the first person who had ever needed Liz.

Even later, after they were married and he hurt her, she knew that he needed her to survive.

Molly's inability to put aside her dislike of Alex bothered Liz. A good friend should just be happy for you. That's what Alex said. He was not immune to Molly's antipathy.

Sometimes Liz would step outside the relationship. She would take a few steps to the side and watch herself and Alex together. In those moments she admitted to herself that it was possible that Molly was right.

Alex told her Molly was 'trashy'. Molly told her Alex was 'strange'.

Liz felt herself pulled both ways and eventually took to keeping them apart. Molly told her she felt 'left behind' and Liz laughed and told her they would always be best friends, but Liz was in love. She stopped needing to shout her opinions in class. Alex didn't like loud abrasive women. She stopped needing to go out and party because it was better when it was just the two of them.

Alex became her world and the little piece of herself that she was keeping safe was chipped away a little bit at a time until Luke was born, and then it was gone forever.

And as the years passed she held on to who he had been but she forgot to hold on to who *she* had been. She felt herself shrink. She was such a tall woman and she took up a lot of space and yet there were times when Alex would walk into a room and call her name because he couldn't see her sitting right there on the couch making herself small.

'At least I've left him now,' she comforted herself.

•

'The important thing to remember, ladies, is that you've taken the biggest step to free yourself. You've left the abuser and you've moved forward with your life. Don't think about how long you stayed. Don't worry about who you were then. Celebrate the woman you are now. Celebrate the strength it took to walk out that door.'

'Should we all get out a mirror and study our vaginas?' said Glenda.

'Yeah, let's find the source of our power,' laughed Rhonda.

'You people are sick,' said Cherry.

'It's better to laugh a little,' Liz said to Rebecca, whose face was flushed with anger.

'I just think we need to stick to the subject,' said Rebecca.

'We live the subject, Rebecca,' said Rhonda. 'No one knows how to stick to the subject more than we do.'

Rebecca had given her a strange look then, like she had something else to say, but then she just shook her head and moved on. Liz had wondered why she was running a domestic violence group at the time. She hardly seemed the type. She blushed a little whenever someone said 'fuck'.

•

Liz toyed with her phone and tried not to look at her mother, who was on the couch knitting a jumper for Luke. It was navy blue with red stripes. Luke only wanted Bob the Builder jumpers these days, but Liz would take the gift and hopefully convince Luke to wear it once or twice.

The knitting kept Ellen away from the whisky. She had cut down on the number of times she went to the bottle standing on the antique wooden trolley but she could not give it up entirely. Everyone had their own ways of getting through the day.

Ellen's needles clicked in the afternoon quiet. The clock in the kitchen ticked away the minutes. Now Alex was twenty-five minutes late. Tick-tock, click-clack.

85

Finally the silence of her mother's unspoken thoughts scratched at Liz. She had watched her mother shake her head as she left her friendly message for Alex. 'Don't give me that, Mum—it's easier if I keep him on side.'

'Are you going to spend the rest of your life placating him, Liz? Are you going to jump every time he wants you to?'

'I've left him, Mum, isn't that enough? I don't have to be rude as well.'

'I hardly think asking him to bring his child back on time could be considered rude, Liz. What are you really worried about? If he tried anything here I would call the police and get his butt hauled off to jail.'

'God, again with the police, Mum? It's not the solution. Do you really want Luke to have a father in prison?'

'No, of course not, but I think you should have gone to the police. You still could go and then at least Luke would know that some behaviours cannot be tolerated. Isn't that important?'

'I don't need to educate Luke about right and wrong, Mum. He's only three years old. He has no real idea what's going on.'

'Really?' said Ellen, and Liz chose to look at the curtains. She wondered if she would seem completely crazy if she got up and moved them aside to peer at the front path.

'What happened to your eye, Mum? What happened to your tummy, Mum? What happened, Mum? What happened?'

'Look, Mum, I can't keep going over this. It will get better with time. I'm sure it will. I don't need to piss him off now, especially when he's out with Luke. I need him to stay sane and calm when he's out with Luke.'

•

'I think I push him sometimes,' said Glenda. 'I make him mad on purpose.'

The women in the group did not respond. Glenda had grabbed the words out of their own heads.

'That's no excuse,' said Rebecca.

'Yeah,' agreed Rhonda nodding, 'no excuse.' But she didn't sound completely convinced.

The logic of the words was hard to accept. Not all women got hit. If you were the one getting a smack maybe you deserved it. That's what he said anyway. The 'he' who hit Glenda and Cherry and Rhonda and Liz and all the other women who drifted in and out of group. That's what 'he' said.

There were ways to avoid being hit. Degrading, debasing ways but there were ways to avoid it. All the women in the group had begged and pleaded their way out once or twice.

•

Liz knew after all these years the things that triggered the rage and she could make sure she avoided them.

Of course, each year the list of triggers got longer and longer and Liz had been able to see a future where everything she did, every breath she took and every sound she made, was a trigger. She had seen a time when there was no way to avoid getting hurt. Leaving had been her way of stopping the list from growing. Now she could control when she saw him, she could pay particular attention to the triggers. He hated to be told what to do, he hated to feel that someone was trying to control his choices, so she arranged her sentences accordingly.

She cringed when she heard herself but everyone knew the truth about old habits.

'He shouldn't bring him back late. He's just doing it to upset you,' said Ellen.

'He's angry. He misses Luke. I might do the same thing if I couldn't see my child.'

'What rubbish—you're still making excuses for him, Liz. You've never said no to him when it comes to Luke. Never.'

Liz said nothing. She got up and moved the curtains aside, ignoring her mother's 'tsk'.

Alex was thirty-eight minutes late.

Her mother had let it be known when she brought Alex home that he was not a choice she respected. Now all Ellen's fears about him had been vindicated. Liz knew there was no point in telling her mother that Alex now was different to Alex then. Her mother had heard it all before. She had seen the signs but she hadn't known how to explain them to Liz. All Liz had seen was this beautiful, clean boy with hair that caught the light and gentle hands. The true Alex had been hiding, waiting for her to let her guard down. Everything he had told her when they were dating sounded different when looked at in the light of what she now knew.

The women who were desperate to be with him and who kept calling had never existed or, if they had, Liz knew that the relationship was the other way around.

He was just so easy to believe. The stories he told about himself had always included some small failing of his that they could both laugh about. She had never had any reason to doubt he had been kicked out of school because he'd been defending himself against a bigger boy whose father donated the library. When he lost the first job he got right out of university she accepted that it was because his boss was a woman who had a thing for him. She understood that in the job he had now he was pressured to go out with the boys and socialise. It was how business worked. Everyone he worked with was 'a regular idiot' or 'up themselves' or 'just trying to cause trouble for me'.

He still looked exactly the same except for the hands. The hands weren't gentle anymore, but if you just looked at him he was still the same boy she had met in the middle of a summer afternoon.

The first time she noticed him the word 'clean' came to mind.

His hair was clean, his clothes were crisp in the heat and there was a lovely smell of soap around him. His teeth were perfect and white and as she handed him his cup of coffee she just knew that here was someone who had never in his whole life been dirty. His nails were shiny and rounded. They could have been the product of a manicure. This was not the kind of man who had ever lifted a piano.

He had come into the coffee shop where she worked. She was reading one of her textbooks and he had to clear his throat to get her attention. Tuesday was her day off from university. Neither of her parents had made it to university. Her father had let her know that she didn't need to work, he would support her all the way through her degree, but Liz enjoyed the coffee shop. It was never busy enough to feel like a real job and she got to have as many cups of coffee as she wanted.

Alex sat around in the coffee shop long after he'd finished his cup of coffee. He just sat at his little table staring at her and pretending to leaf through a magazine every time she caught him at it.

'My manager says you have to buy another cup of coffee or leave.'

'Did he really say that? I didn't know it was the done thing to throw customers out.' His voice was low and deep, as though it came from a man a lot bigger than he was.

'Well you've been here an hour.'

'When does your shift end?'

'Um, I don't really know.'

'Sorry—I'm creeping you out, aren't I? I'm Alex. I've seen you on campus. I'm studying engineering and I think we have a literature class together.'

'If you're studying engineering why are you taking lit?'

'I know, stupid, right? It's part of the course. They seem to think it will make us better communicators in the future if we have a few humanities courses under our belts. Besides, I kind of like it. I'm reading some good books.'

'What did you think of this week's choice?'

'I'm not exactly a fan of Jane Austen but the good thing about her is that there's a movie to go with virtually every book she ever wrote.'

She laughed then. He checked out. He was in her class.

'My shift ends now actually.'

'Well, how about I buy you a cup of coffee or tea? Somewhere else, not here.'

He had a beautiful smile and a deep dimple on his chin. He was shorter than she was and when they left the coffee shop together she rounded her shoulders a little to hide her height.

'I love that you're so tall,' he said without looking at her. 'I love tall women.'

Liz stood up straight and smiled down at him. He wasn't that much shorter than she was.

And that was it, just an ordinary meeting on an ordinary day.

After they had been going out for a few months he told her that he'd first noticed her in class because of her black hair and the way she kept flipping it over her shoulder. Liz wasn't used to being admired from afar. Boys had come and gone but they were only after the same thing. Sometimes she gave in and sometimes she didn't. She was waiting for the one who would make her feel that who she was mattered as much as her large breasts did. She was waiting for someone who actually wanted to love her. And then there was Alex who understood what it was like to have one of your parents leave. Alex, who understood that being loved was not necessarily everyone's right.

And then there was Alex, who ran his fingers through her hair after they had sex and told her she was amazing and that he loved her with everything he had. There was Alex, who wanted to come home to a family. Alex, who needed her to make him feel safe again, the poor boy who had been abandoned by his mother. There was Alex, and Liz was swept up and swept away and she didn't care what her parents thought. She was in love. She held a little bit back because there was no way that she was going to finish up like her mother.

But Alex needed her more than any other man ever had.

Alex was afraid she was going to leave. She would watch him come up the front walk for a date and know that he had changed his shirt three times and shaved twice so his skin would be soft.

For the first time Liz could remember she was in control and she preferred it to always being the one waiting for it to end. She would sit in class and right in the middle of a lecture she would feel her skin tingle like he was actually touching her. Those first few months were coated in honey.

The first time she met his father she'd been somewhat taken aback. His father looked like Alex, with the same build and the same eyes, but there was a bitterness in his words that bothered Liz. He looked up at her just as Alex did and she saw him sneer when he shook her hand. 'You're a big one, aren't you?'

She had been too shocked by the open insult to respond.

'Oh, Dad,' Alex had said, and then he had laughed.

Liz should have said something there and then, but it wasn't polite—and at the time she'd just thought she had been insulted because of her height. She hadn't noticed that Frank had simply declared her a thing.

She told Alex later that he should have admonished his father but Alex had sighed and said, 'My dad's had it hard since my mum left. It can't have been easy being a single father when the whole neighbourhood was still married.'

Liz hung her head then, chastened for her lack of sympathy.

She forgave Alex his few idiosyncrasies, like his perpetual need for order and his way of taking control of where they were going each time they went out and his jealousy when she talked to other men. She forgave him because he was so sweet and so in love with her and he had never had a mother to tell him right from wrong. He brought up the pain of abandonment constantly. If she had been more cynical she might have believed he brought it up a little too often. But she was in love.

His jealousy was almost endearing. 'Why do you and your manager spend so much time laughing?' he asked after waiting for her at the end of a shift one afternoon.

'What do you mean? He told me a joke. It was funny and I laughed.'

'You seem to get on really well with him.'

'I do—he's a nice guy.'

'So do you want to fuck him?'

'Jesus, Alex, where did that come from? He's about ten years older than me. Anyway, I have you; I don't want to fuck anyone else. You're being very weird.'

'Sorry. I'm sorry. It's just that I hate the idea of you being with any other man. I can't help feeling that I'm going to lose you. I already lost one woman who I loved more than anything. I can't lose you as well.'

'You're not going to lose me, Alex. I'm with you.'

'Promise?'

'Promise.'

His strange father was just one more thing to forgive Alex for and it wasn't like they saw him that often. Liz could talk herself out of and around anything if she had to. When her parents' divorce became public knowledge the best she could do was put a positive spin on everything. 'Two birthday presents and two Christmas presents,' she told her friends at school. Her father was a doting daddy who showered her with gifts and her mother was beautiful and so concerned about her that she would never marry again. There was no way she wanted to tell the girls at school who envied her beautiful new clothes and jewellery that her father was good at giving gifts but not at spending time with her or that her mother knocked herself out with whisky every night—sometimes before she cooked dinner.

Alex's father was openly rude to his new partner and refused to discuss his ex-wife. The whole dinner was surreal. Frank didn't talk directly to Liz. Instead he spoke through Alex and he was not shy about his opinions. After the first frustrating hour Liz gave up trying to be included and ate her dinner. Alex and his father had obviously developed their own way of coping after his mother left. It was just the two of them against the world. Liz could understand that.

When they went over to share the news of their engagement Frank had sighed and rubbed at his head.

'You're really young,' he said to Alex.

Alex kept quiet.

Then Barbara said, 'Yes, but you're in love and it's wonderful. Congratulations, you two. Let's have a drink to celebrate.'

They'd had more than a drink and they'd stayed for dinner and two bottles of wine later everyone was completely relaxed.

'Don't let her take over the whole wedding, Alex,' said Frank, pointing his fork at Liz. 'It's your day too. If you have to wear that stupid suit you get involved.'

'It's not really my thing, Dad. Liz can have whatever she wants.'

'Oh, it always starts out that way. Now you're in love and you think you'll never have an argument, but mark my words, boy—put your foot down now.'

'He doesn't have to put his foot down, Mr Harrow,' Liz had said, rousing herself from her alcoholic daze. 'We discuss everything. I respect Alex's opinion and he respects mine.'

Alex's father had looked at her like he was bewildered that she could even speak.

'I put my foot down with this one,' he said, pointing to Barbara, who was stubbing out her second cigarette and refilling her glass with wine. 'Best thing I ever did.'

Liz had raised her eyebrows at Barbara but got nothing back from the woman. She had her wine and cigarettes and Liz could see that Alex's father could say whatever the fuck he liked as long as she had those.

It was another one of those signs she should have noticed.

She wanted to tell her mother about the dinner but she couldn't find a way to talk about it without making Alex look like a dick for not standing up for her, for laughing along at his father's jokes about women.

Ellen's reaction to their engagement had been a tight-lipped smile. Jack had asked her how much the wedding would cost. Alex hadn't been embraced by her family so she reasoned she should expect the same attitude from Frank and Barbara.

In the months leading up to the wedding she occasionally had to bite back the words she wanted to share with her mother. The concerns she wanted to voice didn't gel with the positive image of Alex she tried to present.

Even before she married him Liz knew she had to present the side of Alex she hoped to see rather than the Alex she occasionally worried about. She wanted everyone to have a good opinion of him, even if that meant telling outright lies.

'His father doesn't exactly seem fond of women,' Molly had said after the rehearsal dinner.

'I know, weird, right? I think it's because his wife left him and Alex when Alex was so young.'

'I know, Liz, you told me the story, but his father seems to really dislike us—all of us—and Alex just nods and smiles whenever he spouts his misogynistic bullshit.'

'God, Molly, I've been known to nod and smile when my mother talks crap as well.'

'Yes, but . . .'

'Come on, Molly. I'm getting married tomorrow. Let's have a drink.'

The wedding was perfect although Alex was really angry with the photographer for turning up late. He had been close to hitting the man when his father pulled him away and took him for a drink.

'He just wants everything to be perfect,' Liz told her bridesmaids.

'Yeah,' said Molly. 'He's really into perfect.'

She hadn't wanted to think about it. Alex gave her a pair of diamond earrings and they were going to Bali for their honeymoon. She hadn't wanted to listen. He was so charming, so caring, so concerned about her it was addictive. He was so interested in everything she had to say. If they weren't together he would call her before he went to sleep because, 'I need to hear about your day.'

How could he be anything but perfect for her?

6

Alex told her when they came back from the honeymoon that he thought Molly was a bad influence. Molly wasn't a serious married woman like she was. 'She's always out looking for the next big cock,' he said. Liz could see his point. Molly was all about the parties and who she slept with. When Liz started talking about having a baby Molly had been horrified. 'You're only twenty-four. You've only just got married. You guys need to get to know each other, travel the world. Do stuff.'

Liz had only been able to shake her head at her friend. She wanted a baby. She and Alex wanted a baby. She wouldn't have minded travelling or even working for a few more years but Alex was so into the idea of them being a family. He pointed out babies wherever they went and he had even had a T-shirt made in Bali that said: *Mum and dad went to Bali on their honeymoon and all they got was me.*

At the resort where they were staying he was happy to lie at the pool and just watch families.

'That will be us soon,' he said to Liz whenever some child did something particularly cute. Liz had nodded and smiled and sipped her drink. She was more interested in her magazines.

But by the time they got back from Bali she knew that a baby would make them complete. 'A baby makes you a proper family,' Alex said.

'I want to raise my kids while I'm still young,' she told Molly over coffee. 'I want to travel, but I'd rather travel with my kids, open their eyes to the world. I mean, imagine how amazing it would be to experience different countries through the eyes of your children.'

'Are those your words or Alex's?' said Molly, and Liz had felt herself colour and burn. She had made an excuse about having to get groceries and left the cafe there and then. Molly had called later to apologise.

'I'm sorry, Liz. I have no right to tell you what to do with your life. I'm glad you're so happy.'

'Don't worry about it—and I am happy, Molly. One day you'll meet someone like Alex and you'll know what I mean.'

'Yeah, I guess,' Molly said.

She and Alex had laughed about Molly in bed. Alex said, 'She's just jealous of us, babe. She wants what we've got and she knows there's no man stupid enough to take her on with all her bullshit.'

Liz had agreed with Alex, not wanting to defend her friend when she knew where her loyalty should lie.

She had taken a few steps back from the friendship and concentrated on her marriage. Molly persisted with a few phone calls, but after a while she seemed to give up, and Liz had thought, 'Maybe we weren't that close after all.'

•

Molly never mentioned the visit from Alex that had persuaded her to stop calling her friend.

He had found her in the playground at the school where she taught. It was lunch time and Molly was supervising the children on the play equipment. Alex told the school secretary he was her brother.

At first Molly was worried that something had happened to Liz but Alex just chatted about the weather for a few minutes before letting her know the real reason for his visit.

'I just think it would be better if you gave Liz and me a little space right now,' he said.

Molly had wanted to turn and walk away but she was watching the children and she couldn't. She wanted to tell Alex to just leave but she was out in the open where everyone could see and Molly remembered Alex's stiff fury with the photographer.

'Alex, Liz is my friend. You and I don't need to be friends but you can't dictate who Liz is friends with.'

'Married people compromise, Molly. Maybe you'll never know about that but you wouldn't want to be a reason for Liz and I to fight, would you?'

'Of course not, but she's my friend and I want to spend time with her.'

'Face it, Molly,' Alex said, 'you're in a very different place to Liz. Let her be happy. You want her to be happy, don't you?'

Molly had nodded and even though Alex had smiled the whole time she had been relieved when he left. She had been standing with her arms folded across her chest while they'd been talking. She knew she was protecting herself but she couldn't see what from. Alex had made no threats, yet she had felt threatened.

She did what he asked, deciding that it was better to give Liz the space she needed.

Liz had also, without realising it, taken a few steps back from her parents. She and her father usually saw each other once a month, but one day Liz realised that she had not seen him for two months running. One of the days she was supposed to see him Alex surprised her with a weekend away, and she couldn't say no to that. Then the next time she was supposed to see him Alex had been feeling really sick, complaining of severe pain in his stomach, and Liz really hadn't liked to leave him. When she did see her father there seemed to be less to say and there had never been very much to talk about anyway.

Alex liked to hear about all the ways her parents had betrayed her. If she mentioned something about them that irritated her he would agree and give her more examples to mull over. Liz could feel herself handing up her parents' quirks to Alex like a gift. He was always so happy when she had something unflattering to say about her mother or her father. He would jump into the discussion with relish, pointing out things she may have missed.

'We're fine, just the two of us,' Alex said. 'We don't need anyone else and one day there'll be a baby and we will be a real family. It will be nothing like the families we came from.'

She was working during the day teaching a class of seven-year-olds and there was a lot of stuff to do in the house after school.

'How many times do you really need to see your mother?' Alex asked.

'Your mother is always making snide remarks about me and my father,' Alex said.

'You mother hates me. I bet she wishes we would get divorced. She would rather have you alone and unhappy than with me,' Alex pouted.

Liz could laugh at some of the stuff he said. She could deny her mother felt that way and she could tell him to get over it, but as time passed it was easier to see her mother less and lie about it when she did.

She spent more time on the house and more time being a good wife.

Alex liked things done a certain way and she was okay with that. 'My father and I had to keep order after she left or everything would have been complete chaos,' he told her.

'You were only five,' she said. 'How could you keep things in order?'

'I just did what had to be done,' he said.

Something in his voice broke her heart. She knew what a five-year-old boy was like. Some of the ones at school hadn't quite figured out toilet training. They cried for their mothers without a second thought and greeted them like long-lost lovers at the end of the day. She wanted to shed tears for five-year-old Alex but something in his tone made her restrain herself. He was allowed to bring up his mother, but she was not.

Their first anniversary came and went and without her being totally conscious of what had happened; Liz structured her whole life around keeping Alex happy.

She was very good at keeping him happy until Luke arrived. Then she had someone more important to keep happy and Alex hadn't liked that. He hadn't liked that at all. She wanted to tell him that this was how mothers were with their children but she couldn't think of how to say it.

She did start to wonder why his mother had left. Frank was a difficult man but that couldn't be the full story, and it was possible that he had been easy-going and happy before his wife left. After Luke arrived she could not imagine ever leaving him. The concept of walking out on your child was ridiculous. Why hadn't Alex's mother just taken him with her? She couldn't ask these questions of Alex.

She left the past where it was. If Alex didn't want to get in touch with his mother then it was not Liz's business to figure things out for him. She felt the baby kick and she stopped thinking about anything else. She wanted the perfect marriage and the perfect family as much as Alex did. Every book, every television show and every internet forum on marriage told her it was all about compromise. That's what she did—until what she was required to compromise was everything.

•

Liz turned away from the window and went into the kitchen to make another cup of tea. While she was waiting for the kettle to boil she chewed on a fingernail. Alex was forty-five minutes late now. Forty-five minutes was nothing. There was really no reason to be worried except . . . except . . . except lateness was not something Alex tolerated.

When they started dating he always rang the bell exactly on time and he made little remarks about women being ditzy when it came to time because she was always just a few minutes behind. Sometimes she had to change and sometimes her hair wasn't working. Her lateness became a running joke that had an edge to it she hadn't appreciated at first. To Alex, her inability to be on time meant that she had little chance of controlling other areas of her life.

'Not sure how you can keep a class of little kids on the straight and narrow when you won't be there as the bell rings,' he had joked.

'Don't let Liz organise tonight or we'll never get there,' he told his friends.

'Just tell Liz a time about fifteen minutes before she actually needs to be there and then we're golden.'

Eventually she did exactly what he wanted; she got ready early enough to watch him walk up the front path and early enough to be ready to leave as soon as she opened the door.

Alex was never early and he was never late. It was just the way he was. Since the day they had separated, Alex had always brought Luke back on time. In chat rooms she read about how infuriating it was for other women whose ex-husbands were late picking up the kids and late dropping them off and she had always been pleased that at least this was not one of her concerns.

Something was different. If she didn't try to ignore the niggling concern, she was beginning to feel she knew that today was very different. Last night had given Alex some hope and this morning she had taken it away from him. There was no question that she shouldn't have done that but she had and now he was late.

She looked at her watch again. It was two forty-seven. She poured herself a cup of tea and noticed her hand was trembling. She thought about getting in her car to go and look for them but she had no idea where she would even begin.

When the phone rang her heart leapt in her chest and she grabbed it so clumsily she almost dropped it.

'Hey, babe,' said Alex.

'Alex, Jesus, where are you? You're so late. He's missed his nap time.' Fear made her louder than she should have been. She couldn't explain why she was scared. It was a creeping knowledge that was coming with each passing minute that they weren't home. She pissed him off immediately.

'Calm the fuck down, Liz. I thought we could spend a little more time together. He's having such fun.'

'Where are you?'

'We're at one of those arcade places. I don't really know where. Some shopping centre I guess. Anyway, he's having a great time. He's with his dad. Come here, Luke; tell Mum you're having a good time.'

Liz could hear the metallic ringing noises usually associated with arcades. Luke loved them but they were a once-in-a-while treat. The flashing lights always gave Liz a headache. There were only a few games for his age and he always sulked about not being able to play everything. Mostly he just liked to feed the tokens into the machines. She felt momentarily grateful that Alex had taken him and she could put it off herself for a few months.

'Hi, Mum,' said Luke.

'Hey, baby boy, are you okay?'

'Yeah, but Dad took my blankie. He says big boys don't have blankies.'

Liz could hear the tremor in Luke's voice. He was trying not to cry. Alex was very into the idea that big boys didn't cry. He had been saying it to Luke since Luke could talk. She told her son that it was okay to cry sometimes and that she would keep it a secret when he did. Now she felt his little voice pull at her heart and she wanted to reach through the phone and grab him away from his father. She could feel an acid growl start in her stomach. She bit down on her tongue, keeping herself calm, keeping Luke calm.

'No, that's not true. Big boys can have blankies. Don't worry. You can have it when you get home. I promise.'

'Okay.'

Alex took the phone from his son. 'Stop turning him into a wuss, Liz. The kid is too big to have a blankie.'

'Alex, where are you? Tell me the name of the shopping centre. I can drive out and meet you. Save you the drive back.'

'I don't know the name, Liz. It's not near your mother's house. We've been driving around.'

Alex knew the name. Why was he lying?

'But if you just ask someone I could . . .'

'No, Liz, I don't want you to fetch him. He's with me now. Do you understand? He's with me.'

Liz could hear that something had shifted. Alex's voice had dropped a tone. He was waiting for her to say something wrong. He wanted her to push him. He wanted her to give him an excuse. She just didn't know what he needed an excuse for.

'Okay, Alex. But you need to bring him home now, it's way past two.'

'I told you, babe—we're having a bit more time together. He's my kid, Liz. You can't tell me how much time I'm allowed to spend with him.' Liz could hear a smile in his voice. Not a smile—a smirk. He was a cat with a silly little mouse to play with.

'I know, Alex; I'm not trying to tell you anything. I just don't want him to get too tired. You know how cranky he can get.'

'He's fine when he's with me, Liz. I don't take crap. I want you to talk to me for a few minutes. We need to sort this thing out. Before I bring him back I want a proper answer from you. I need to know if you're going to come home. Home where you belong.'

Liz understood now, but she had to stay strong. She would not tell Alex what he wanted to hear.

'Alex, I've told you I need time to figure things out. Please—now is not the time to talk. Bring Luke home and I promise I'll make a time with you when we can discuss things.'

'Do you think I'm stupid, Liz?' Alex's voice was low and menacing. Liz's body recognised the change before her mind did. Her muscles went stiff and she braced herself for the physical contact, but she wasn't with him.

He couldn't hit her, so who was he going to hit?

Who was he going to hit?

She thought about Luke and the possibility that he might get in the way of Alex's simmering rage but then she shook her head. Alex wouldn't hurt Luke—he just wouldn't.

'Alex, I'm sorry. Of course I don't think you're stupid. I know we have to discuss this, I know we do. Maybe you're right. You come home now and I can let my mother take Luke out for dinner. We can go out or stay here, just the two of us, and we can talk.'

'You say that now, Liz, but as soon as I get there you're going to fob me off and whine about needing more time. That's always the way it is with you.'

'I know we need to talk, Alex. Just come home and we'll have all the time we need to discuss this.'

It would have been easy just to say yes to him, but when he brought Luke home she didn't want to have to deal with his anger when she told him she had lied.

'*Bing!* Did you hear that, Liz?'

'What?'

'*Bing!* Time's up, Liz. Time's up.'

And then the phone went dead.

For a moment Liz just stood and looked at the phone in her hand. She didn't even know what to think. She didn't understand what he meant by 'time's up'.

He had never hung up on her before. She was the one who usually ended their calls: 'I can't discuss this anymore, Alex. I'll call you tomorrow.'

She should have lied. She should have told him that they could play happy families again.

She would tell him right now. She dialled the phone, ready with her lie, but it went straight to voicemail. He had switched it off again.

She called back three or four times and then she gave up.

Alex wasn't winding himself up; he was already taut and ready to snap. She could feel it.

He needed her to use a word or a phrase or a tone that he could hang on to and then use as an excuse. She rubbed her head trying to think of what he had in mind. What was he going to do and blame her for later? Would he hit Luke? Could he actually strike his three-year-old child with the same force he used to hit her?

She wished he was there with her now. She would say something, anything, and snap the elastic. If she was there he could hit her. At least after he hit her she didn't have to wait for it anymore. Once it was over she could take comfort in his kind words and promises and know that at least for a day or a week she was safe. After a week at the most she would see a change in

Alex, just something small in the way he looked at her and she would know that the cycle was beginning again.

The waiting was harder than the pain.

While she was waiting she was always working out how hard it was going to be and how much damage was going to be done. She was already preparing her excuses for the outside world should anyone other than Alex catch a glimpse of the damage to her flesh.

Liz had never been very good at the waiting. There had been times when the waiting had been too hard and then she had pushed and goaded and laughed at Alex so that the wait would be over. There had been times when it had been her fault, even though it was never supposed to be her fault. Presumably there were women who were better at the waiting. Liz always wondered if they got hit less.

Even though Liz only ever traced the abuse back to after Luke had been born, there had been a time before Luke. A time when she was still firmly entrenched in the first flush of love. It was something she couldn't tell anyone about. The incident made her cringe when she thought about it now.

They had only been going out for a few months when they decided to have a weekend away together. Liz had arrived at Alex's apartment to find him methodically filling his suitcase with neat piles of clothing. He was muttering to himself as he packed, reminding himself of everything he needed to take with him, and Liz had found him so peculiar she had laughed. He had laughed with her and then, after watching him for a few more minutes, she began to tease him.

'Careful there, Alex, I think your underwear and your socks may have mixed a little in that corner.'

'Watch out, Alex, I don't think that shirt is perfectly straight.'

She couldn't quite pick the moment when he had stopped laughing but it was only a moment between him laughing and him picking up a perfectly rolled pair of socks and throwing it at her. It was only a pair of socks but they had hit her in the eye with an unnerving accuracy. He hadn't hurt her, not really. It was a pair of socks and her eye felt a bit strange and there were a few stinging tears but it wasn't like she was in pain.

'Oh, God, Liz, I'm so sorry, I don't know what happened . . . it was a joke. I'm sorry. I didn't mean to actually hit you.'

She had forgiven him. Of course she had forgiven him. It was only a pair of socks.

That night, after they had made love and he had drifted off to sleep in the big hotel bed, she had tried to figure out why the incident had disturbed her so much. It could have been the precision with which the socks were thrown or it could have been something else she had noticed. Alex had apologised again and again and he had continually asked if she was okay as they made their way to the hotel, but there was something else underneath all his concern that bothered her. In the moment between the socks hitting her eye and Alex apologising, Liz had seen him look at her with a small flicker of amazed triumph. He had hurt her and he had seemed, only for a moment, to be proud of the fact that he could hurt her. It was a bizarre understanding that she came to. She couldn't discuss the incident with anyone because it was only a pair of socks, a rolled-up ball of cotton. People would probably laugh at her.

If she thought about it the right way, if she blamed herself enough, then just about every incident was just an accident.

The first time Alex had really hurt her he was trying to get past her in the middle of an argument over her bringing Luke into the bed at night, and he had shoved her a little. Well, more than a little. She had been standing in front of the bedroom door at the time and the round brass doorknob had pressed deeply into her back. Luke was only two months old and she felt like death would be a solution to her sleep problems. Someone suggested co-sleeping and Liz finally got a few hours in between feeds but Alex hated sharing his bed with the baby. She would curl her body protectively around Luke and he felt excluded.

The doorknob had left a purple circle on her back. It was the first time it had ever happened. Before Luke arrived there were times when she felt him getting close to an explosion but then she could always prevent it. She had no idea why she wanted to prevent it. She told herself it was love and that she didn't want him to be unhappy. She told herself that marriage was about compromise. Alex was big on the word 'compromise'.

After Luke was born she was just so tired that she didn't see the telltale signs that she'd pushed him too far. She couldn't dredge up the energy to distract him with sex or cook him his favourite dinner or just talk him out of his anger.

He had been so apologetic that first time. He had asked to see the bruise again and again and then cursed himself for marking her flesh. Something about the way he looked at the bruise had felt familiar but she couldn't think what.

She hadn't remembered the sock incident then.

He had brought her flowers and cooked dinner and walked the hallway with Luke for hours so that she could sleep. Liz had wanted to talk things through and maybe get Alex to agree to talk to someone about how he was feeling but she didn't really have the energy. She was too tired, too grateful for his apology. It was only later, after she had left him and spent the nights at her mother's house trapped in the chat rooms of the abused, that she remembered about the socks and it occurred to her that each time he hurt her there was a moment that she saw if she was watching him: the moment when he was pleased that he had managed to hurt her.

She had laughed out loud at the memory of the socks and then, when she realised that it had been the biggest sign of them all, she had cried.

He was always brilliant in the loving phase. The phase that came after the tension phase and the explosion phase was the best time to be married to Alex.

'After he broke my arm the first time he got me a car,' said Rhonda. *'It was a piece of shit but at least I could get to the shops.'*

'He took the kids for three days so I could go on a girl's weekend after he gave me two black eyes,' said Cherry.

'He let me get pregnant again and he didn't touch me the whole time after he punched me in the stomach and I lost the first one,' said Glenda.

It took her a long time to see the pattern. Men who really beat their wives weren't so sorry after it happened, were they? She didn't dare look it up on their shared computer and there was no way she would give either of her parents the satisfaction of such a discussion.

When she had joined the group and listened to the other women talk sentimentally about the loving phase and all that came with it she had felt completely stupid. She was an educated woman but she had imagined that such a thing could not possibly happen to her.

She kept quiet, she made excuses for him, she blamed herself and she learned to be very, very good. She moved Luke out of their bed and lay still while Alex climbed on top of her and Luke screamed. She asked him about his day first before she told him about her day. She cooked his favourite foods and pushed pieces of meat past her lips because he liked company while he ate. She did all the right things but somehow she still managed to make him angry enough to hurt her. The list of triggers was growing longer and longer.

Some days she thought she had seen all the triggers but then a new one would pop up which she only noticed when she was nursing a bruise. Unfolded washing had become a trigger on a day when the rest of the house was perfect. The laundry basket sat on top of the washing machine in the laundry. He'd had to go looking for it because the laundry was at the back of the house but he'd found it and he had added it to his list and the bruise on the top of Liz's arm had taken days to fade. The next day he came home with takeaway food and a bunch of roses. He seemed to think it was a fair trade and she had smiled and accepted his apology again.

When she had finally taken down the suitcase when he was at work and crept out of the house her mother had been horrified.

'You never let a man put his hands on you, Liz. Didn't I tell you that over and over again?'

Liz had merely nodded at her mother. If you weren't in it you couldn't understand it.

'At least you left him the first time he did it,' her mother had said, little knowing it was far from the first time. It was just the first time that the bruises couldn't be hidden.

Liz had known after he punched her in the face because the chicken was overdone that they were moving into a new stage. If he didn't care who saw what he had done then she was in real trouble.

After his fist had connected with her face Alex had said, 'Go show that to your mother,' and then he had gone out to get himself some proper dinner.

In the morning he had been horrified at the damage he had caused. He had begged, literally begged her to stay inside until she was healed. He would do everything. He would stay home and take care of Luke so she could rest. He would cook and clean.

He told her he was ashamed of himself. He even shed a tear or two. She had accepted his grief and his shame and his pleas for her to forgive him and told him that she would be fine. She would stay at home until she was ready for the world again. She told him to go to work and he could call all day to find out how she was doing. She mentioned his boss, who was 'an arsehole', and he smiled at her for remembering how important it was for him to stay on top of things at work. He told her he loved her and that she was the perfect wife and mother and that he was going to be better. He was going to do better.

Even nodding hurt but Liz had nodded to let him know that she understood.

Once he had left the house she had known what needed to be done. She and Luke made a game of packing for a holiday at

Nana's house. They packed quickly in order to leave before the first phone call so that Luke would not give anything away. Alex always asked to speak to Luke. He always got Luke to tell him what Mummy had been doing.

So they packed and Luke touched her black eye gently with his chubby little hands and wondered how she had hurt herself and Liz looked at her son and knew she had to pack faster and leave quicker.

Because always, every time something happened, the idea that Luke might one day be included in his rages was there. Luke was always clean, just sleepy enough to give no trouble and adoring when his father came home. But Liz knew she couldn't control his behaviour forever.

Alex loved his son more than anything. His absolute adoration of his child was the right way for him to feel about Luke but he was wary about Liz feeling the same way about the boy.

'There are two boys in your life, Liz,' he said. 'Remember that.'

But Luke was getting bigger. He had some distinctly unlovable moments like every child did. He wanted to stay up and play and sometimes he wanted his toys out of their boxes and strewn across his bedroom floor. Sometimes he wanted to jump when it was time to lie down, and he could shout and cry when he got angry. Liz saw the possibility of Luke testing his father. And Luke had no idea where that could lead. Alex had called her before she got

Luke out of the house but by then Luke knew they were keeping a secret surprise from daddy. A wonderful secret surprise.

'Me and mum are playing dress-ups,' Liz heard him say into the phone. Just the way she had told him to say it.

The second time Alex called Liz had told him that Luke's hands were covered with paint, and by the third time they were safe in her mother's house and Liz was bracing for the moment when Alex walked back into an empty house.

She had spent the first two weeks at her mother's house just waiting for Alex to break down the door and drag her home again. It was only when she realised that he had little or no strength in the outside world—in the light, where people could see him—that she could finally relax.

•

He couldn't touch her now because she had moved out of his house. He couldn't hurt her because she didn't live with him and now Liz wondered as she stared at the phone in her hand if that meant he needed to find another way to hurt her. Did he miss the feeling of triumph he got after he threw the socks and pushed her into a door and punched her in the eye? And if he missed it, what would he do to get it back?

How far would he go?

Now she dialled his phone one more time. If he would only answer she would use the right words. She would say whatever she needed to say. She would suggest she come and meet them and they could do something together as a family. Alex wanted them to be a family again and she could play along with the best of them. There was a deep feeling of unease taking over her body. She wasn't there for Alex to take out his rage on. There was only one person there he could hurt and that was Luke. As she dialled his number she finally allowed herself to acknowledge her worst fear: that Alex was capable of hurting his son in order to hurt her.

Alex's phone was still switched off.

She went into the lounge room.

'We need to call the police again,' she told her mother. Her stomach rolled over and she could feel beads of sweat forming on her face. Her heart was racing. What did they call this? Animal instinct.

Something was very wrong.

If she had to put her fear into words she knew it would sound silly. She could call the police station and say, 'My husband is late bringing back my son and I'm really worried because he took his blankie away and he knows how important that blankie is to Luke. He was the one who bought it for him. After I found out I was pregnant I called Alex and that very night he came home with this blue blanket edged in satin that was so soft it made me want to cry. I wrapped our son in it when he came home from the hospital and we had to search the internet to find two or three more because he could never sleep without his blankie.

I keep one at my mother's house and one in the car just in case he needs to touch something to feel safe and now his father has taken it away. I'm worried because I think that if he's taken away the blankie he's trying to make him grow up and I know what my husband does to grownups who piss him off.'

'Don't wait, Liz,' said her mother. In Ellen's concerned gaze Liz could see her own fear reflected. 'Don't wait any longer, just call them.'

Ellen had put down her knitting. Her hands began a dance, twisting and turning as they sought the glass that would hold something to make this moment and all moments to come easier.

Liz wanted her mother to tell her to relax, to calm down and have another cup of tea. She wanted her to say, 'You can't get this hysterical every time he's late bringing Luke back.'

But her mother said, 'Call them.'

Liz felt like she was riding a sea of nausea when she picked up the phone.

She dialled the police station again.

Something was very wrong.

One hour late

'Good afternoon, West Wood police station, can I help you?'

'Yeah, um, I called a while ago about my son. He's out with his father on an access visit and they're not home yet.'

'How long ago did you call, ma'am?'

'I called at about twenty past two.'

Lisa looked at her watch.

'Okay, ma'am, can you give me your full name and your son's name and your husband's name again?'

The woman on the phone talked and Lisa wrote down the details again and compared them to the last call.

She hadn't done anything about the first call. The phone had not stopped and when it finally quietened down some woman came in with a broken nose and bled everywhere while she screamed about the 'fucker' who had hit her.

It crossed Lisa's mind that she should have done something but she let the thought go. There was no point in looking back because there was nothing she could have done anyway. She took a deep breath and sent up a little prayer to the heavens that this was still just an ordinary day.

'Okay, Liz—can I call you Liz?'

'Yes, sure, that's fine.'

'You need to come in so we can discuss this further.'

'No . . . no I can't leave. If they come back . . . I need to be here.'

'You really need to come in, Liz. That way we can raise our level of concern.'

'I can't come in. I'm not leaving this house.'

The woman sounded stubbornly attached to the idea of remaining at home.

'Is there anyone else out looking for them?'

'No, we haven't—I mean . . . I'm going to call . . . I'm going to call my father. He could go out to look but we have no idea where they are.'

'Could your father stay at the house and wait for them while you come in and file the report?'

'No, I told you: I can't leave. If he comes home and finds me gone it will piss him off.'

'Who will it piss off, Liz?'

'Alex. It will upset Alex and I've already . . .'

'You've already what, Liz?'

'Nothing. I just don't want to come in and I want my parents here with me. I need to stay here!'

'Okay, Liz, it's okay. I need you to stay calm so we can sort this out. Don't yell at me and I won't yell at you and we can talk this through.'

'Sorry, I'm sorry . . . I'm just . . .'

'I know, Liz. I understand. Okay now . . . tell me when you last spoke to Alex.'

'He just called now.'

'And where did he say they were?'

'At an arcade, at a shopping centre. He didn't seem sure which shopping centre.'

'He didn't seem sure? Was he upset? Did he sound agitated?'

'No . . . Well, yeah, I guess. He sounded angry.'

'He sounded angry?'

'Yes.'

'Who is he angry with?'

'Me, of course. He wants to reconcile and I don't. I didn't want to discuss getting back together again. I just wanted him to bring Luke home.'

'Did you talk to your son?'

'I did and he's okay. It's just a feeling I have. He's very late and he usually brings Luke back on time. In fact, he's always on time. Time is a big thing for Alex. He hates to be late.'

'Okay, Liz, I know I asked you before but I need to ask again: is there any reason why you are concerned about your husband and son being late?'

'Well, he's an hour late now. That's pretty late.'

'Okay.'

'Look, I know it sounds stupid but he switched off the phone after we talked and he seemed really angry. He says he wants more time with my son, with Luke, but I'm worried that he might decide to keep him or something.'

'Why do you think he would do that, Liz?'

'I don't know. He's angry about the separation and he has a temper.'

'Ding, ding, ding,' thought Lisa. 'And there it is.'

'Has he ever harmed you or Luke?'

'Not Luke—he's never hurt Luke.'

'But he's hurt you?'

'Yes.'

Lisa took a deep breath. The woman on the phone said 'yes' and that 'yes' could mean anything. It could mean that her husband hurled ugly words at her occasionally. It could mean that sometimes if he wanted sex and she said 'not tonight' she wound up doing what he wanted after he pushed her down and held her there. It could mean he gave her a little slap with an open hand or a punch with a closed fist, or it could mean that every now and then he put her in the hospital.

Two months ago she had been out on duty when there was a domestic violence call. She and Max had been working together then, and when they had arrived they found the wife barricaded in the bedroom, refusing to come out. 'Has your husband hurt you?' Max had asked and the woman had said 'yes' through the door. Just one word. Just 'yes'.

Eventually, when she was sure he was handcuffed and the ambos had arrived, the woman had opened the door.

Lisa had to hold on to her stomach when she saw her. One arm dangled uselessly by the woman's side and there were bleeding cuts all over her face. Three of her teeth were missing and her leg collapsed out from under her when she tried to walk. They had asked if her husband had hurt her and all she had said was 'yes'.

Lisa knew that there were so many possible scenarios behind a 'yes' she couldn't even begin to count them. She gave herself a small mental kick for not asking the woman the last time she had called.

'I wish you'd mentioned that earlier,' she said.

'It's not something . . . I didn't know it would be relevant.'

'Yes,' said Lisa. 'It's very relevant.' She was angry now. 'When was the last time you suffered abuse at the hands of your husband?'

There was silence on the other end of the phone. It was a humiliating question to have to answer.

'If you are serious about your concern, Mrs Harrow, you are going to have to give me some more information.'

'About five months ago,' said the woman.

'And what happened then?'

'He gave me a black eye.'

'He punched you in the eye?'

'Yes, he said the chicken was overdone.' The woman's voice was flat.

There was no official reason to do anything. But the woman needed help. Lisa knew that she needed help.

'Fine,' said Lisa. 'Give me your address. I'm going to send over someone to talk to you.'

'Okay,' said Liz. 'Okay, thanks very much. Thanks.'

Lisa could hear the woman's tears down the line.

'Fuck,' she thought as she put down the phone. The woman should have told her the real situation before. She would have done something. They could have begun actively searching. What was it with these women? Why, even after they had to walk around with a black eye and get themselves an AVO, did they still try to protect the bastard who hurt them? The woman should have come to the police before she separated from him. She should have got a lawyer involved and the system and then there would be no way the guy would be allowed to see the kid alone. Now look where they were. Legally Lisa didn't have to do anything until the woman filed a report but something in her voice told

Lisa this was the time to follow her instinct. This woman knew something was wrong. Lisa would bet she was still holding back some information.

She typed *Alex Harrow* into the computer but nothing came up.

It could mean one of two things: either the woman was bullshitting and her ex had never laid a hand on her, or she had never reported him at all. A lot of stuff got said when people split up, so she couldn't discount the bullshitting option was probably the truth but just in case she would ask Rob to go by.

Rob would be happy to go.

It had been a slow day so far.

So far.

•

Senior Constable Robert Williams was in the back picking his teeth with a mangled paper clip. He hated days when there was nothing to do but wait for some crazy person to call. He was glad he hadn't been the one to drive out to the dispute over Aunty Thelma's necklace.

He had just put down the phone on Natalie, claiming an emergency.

'I believe you do that whenever you don't want to finish our discussions,' she said.

'Natalie, I'm a police officer. I have work to do. I'm telling you that I can't afford to pay for soccer for Mark this month.'

'He's only six, Robert, and all his friends are doing it.'

'Well maybe all his friends' fathers aren't cops trying to support two households. Why don't you get you super boyfriend to pay for it?'

'Oh fuck off, Robert—Mark isn't his kid.'

'Well then I guess Mark isn't going to play soccer this year—and, may I add, fuck off to you too.'

The phone had clicked in his ear and he had sighed. The arguments between him and Natalie seemed to be getting more infantile with each passing month. He could quite possibly see a time when they would just stick their tongues out at each other instead of exchanging actual words. Divorce was supposed to get easier when all the papers were signed and everyone knew how things worked but it just seemed to be getting harder. He knew that Natalie would make sure that Mark was aware his father was the reason he couldn't play soccer this season, but there was nothing he could do. Between the uniform and the boots and registration he was up for close to five hundred dollars and this month he needed to get the credit card sorted. Mark would understand. He would look at him with his big brown eyes and say, 'It's okay, Dad. I can wait.'

Fuck, the kid was only six years old. Sometimes he sounded older than his father. Kids shouldn't have to deal with their parents' bullshit but there was no way for them to avoid it. It was hard to believe that Natalie once thought he was the greatest man in the world. Now she just thought he was a waste of space who couldn't afford to pay for soccer. He knew she was hurting as well when she couldn't give the kids everything they wanted. He knew she was just as upset as he was, but somehow that understanding disappeared when they spoke to each other. After ten years of marriage and three kids all they seemed to have left was 'fuck you' and 'fuck you too'. It was pretty pathetic and goddamn sad.

The door opened and Lisa peered in. 'I think you need to take a run out to this house,' she said.

'What is it?'

'A woman on the phone, Elizabeth Harrow, says her husband is late bringing back the kid.'

'How late?'

'It's only an hour now but she seems pretty concerned.'

'Why didn't you tell her to come in?'

'I did; she doesn't want to leave the house. But . . .'

'But what?'

'Something's wrong, Rob. I think you need to get over there.'

Robert rubbed his face and looked at Lisa. Right now their relationship was uncomplicated, both of them filling a physical need, but whenever they talked he was aware that Lisa had good police instincts. They had her on the desk a lot because she could hear changes in tone and fear in the voices of the people who called. She knew when to prioritise a case. If she said something was wrong he was inclined to believe her.

'There a history of violence?'

'She says so.'

'Shit,' said Robert. A history of violence couldn't be ignored. 'Do you think she's telling the truth?'

'I don't know,' said Lisa. She rubbed her head and then she took the clip that was holding her hair in place out and tidied it before clipping it up again. Robert knew it was what she did when she was thinking something through.

'She must be worried,' he thought as his eyes roamed over her heart-shaped face and rested on her breasts for a moment.

'I could be wrong, Rob, but there's something about this. It feels . . . it feels a little familiar.'

Robert didn't need to ask what she meant. She had been down in Melbourne when some dickhead had stabbed his toddler and then put it up on Facebook. The mother had called the police but by the time they found the kid she was already dead. Lisa wasn't directly involved in the case but they'd had to roll out the counsellors for months afterwards.

'Okay,' said Rob, standing up. 'I'll get over there now. Call Dave for me and let him know we need to go. I think he's gone to get some lunch.'

'Will do,' said Lisa.

Robert slipped his hand to his side and felt for the gun which he knew would be there. Twenty years on and he still automatically checked it before he did anything else.

This was probably just going to be some woman pissed off at her husband for keeping the kid out a little later than she said he could. He would bet there was no history of violence either, but you never knew and everything had to be checked out.

Parents ran off with their kids all the time and then the whole thing became a manhunt and the kid involved always suffered more that the parents, who were just trying to find a way to hurt someone else as much as they felt they'd been hurt.

Sometimes they did worse than run away. That guy who threw his kid off the bridge didn't give anyone any warning, but the one who stabbed his toddler to death let the kid call home and tell her mother she loved her. A true fucking gentleman.

People were truly fucked in the head. Every year Robert thought that he'd seen it all and every year people lowered the bar a little further. It wasn't like he didn't know how angry you could get with your ex-wife. Natalie made him want to spit fire sometimes, but the kids were more important than they were. He knew that and Natalie knew it. They argued quietly over the phone, mostly about money, and let the kids think the divorce had been amiable. He didn't understand these guys who killed their kids to get back at their wives. He loved his kids as much as Natalie did. If he hurt them he would be hurting himself.

What pushed someone over the edge and into that dark place where their desire to hurt someone clouded every other rational thought?

They had been told last month to take these cases seriously. Even if the person on the phone seemed to be a fruit loop looking for entertainment they had to look into it.

No one wanted to be the one who'd missed it when some guy left the country with his kids in tow or worse.

Dave came into the station as Robert was putting his mobile into his pocket.

'Lisa filled me in. You ready?'

'Ready,' said Robert. Dave smelled like he'd had Indian food for lunch. The man never worried about what he put in his mouth. Robert's sushi was meant to keep his weight under control but he would much rather have had Indian, especially when he had to share a car with Dave.

They made their way out to their car.

'Seems like we get one of these every second day,' said Dave, filling the car with the smell of chicken korma.

'Yep,' agreed Robert.

'I'm never getting married,' he said as he keyed the address into the GPS.

'You think that,' said Robert, 'and then along comes a woman who seems like she was just made to slot perfectly into your life. She's the yin to your yang and all that other crap and before you know it you're picking out matching towels for the guest bathroom.'

'Fuck that,' said Dave. 'Every time one of them gets too close I let them know it's time for me to move on.'

Robert laughed. 'When you fall, Dave, you're going to fall hard.'

7

Alex put the phone in his pants pocket, pushing it down hard. Burying her and her bullshit.

How many times had he said sorry? Twenty, maybe thirty times? He apologised with flowers and with chocolates and he'd even sent her a bracelet through the mail. What more did she want from him? He was sick of all this crap. If she didn't want to come home then she shouldn't have flashed her pussy at him. What was last night about?

God, his father had been so right. Women didn't know how to forgive you.

They held on to your past mistakes and twisted them over the phone to their mothers and their friends and then all of a sudden one innocent little shove became abuse. He knew how it happened. He saw it all the time. Men were always thrown in the shit and blamed for every fucking thing that went wrong. At work his friend Greg had been kicked out by his wife for sleeping with one of the secretaries. Greg was sorry he'd screwed up and he seemed to be on the phone every other day begging his wife to take him back. Alex told him he needed to let his wife know that he'd only had sex with someone else because she had a permanent headache. Greg just shook his head when Alex talked to him. The man was so completely whipped it was embarrassing to watch him. Was that what Liz wanted from him?

He could feel her pulling further and further away. In the last few months they hadn't spent more than five minutes on the phone when he called. She was trying to turn raising their son into some sort of business. She sent him emails and then when he came to get Luke she had always just stepped out for a minute or just got into the shower and he was left looking at Ellen, who didn't even try to pretend she liked him.

And then there had been last night, when he had seen it all fall back into place again. He knew she couldn't resist him in daddy mode and he had wanted to see Luke. He had been reading him the last story and he had looked up and seen her standing in the doorway watching them. His heart had soared then because he knew that she was seeing what a good dad he was. He knew she was missing that as much as he missed his time with Luke.

Now she was trying to back away, to make last night a mistake. She was trying to break his heart again. Well, he'd told her now. Time was up. He was sick of waiting for her to make a decision. He was tired of walking around with this black dog sitting on his chest. That's what they called it these days—a black dog. Alex could picture the creature. He was a giant slobbering beast with razor-sharp teeth and foul breath and he wouldn't budge. He had taken up residence the day Liz left, the day his world—the world he had created—had ended.

When he had come home from work to find them gone he had driven straight over to her mother's house and pounded on the door until Liz opened it. She had lied to him when she told him she understood and that she forgave him. She had lied when she said she wouldn't leave the house and she had lied when she said she wouldn't tell anyone what had happened.

On the day she left he had called her from work to apologise even though he wasn't exactly sure it was all his fault. He hated dry chicken. He told her that again and again and she just didn't listen. It wasn't even just dry, it was practically inedible, and she'd just whined at him about Luke catching his finger in the door. The kid was fine. Rushing him to the doctor like some neurotic woman was just a waste of time. How hard could it be to get it right? All she had to do all day was take care of Luke and make a fucking edible dinner. He knew he had hurt her, that he shouldn't have gotten so angry, so he'd called to apologise.

In his defence it had been a shitty time at work. His new boss was a complete arsehole and Tim, who was supposed to be checking everything, had failed to find a whole lot of mistakes in their latest project. He had tried to explain to the man that it was all Tim's fault but the dickhead hadn't wanted to listen and then Tim was spreading all this shit around the office about how he lied and hadn't finished the work he was supposed to get done. So it had been a bad day and then he had to come home to a rubbish meal and he'd just lost it.

So of course he knew that she needed an apology. He had called home, as he arrived at work the next day, to say that he was sorry. In fact he had called every hour that morning, just to check that she was okay. He had gone out when he was supposed to be in a lunch meeting and ordered a huge bunch of flowers to be delivered to the house as soon as possible. He ordered yellow roses because she loved yellow roses and then the girl behind the counter told him she could include a box of handmade chocolates for only ten dollars more and he had told her to go ahead and do that.

'Your wife is a very lucky woman,' the girl had said, giving him one of those sexy smiles that told him she was into him and Alex had nodded, knowing that it was the truth.

He had felt better after that and he even managed to sort out some problems with the project so the wanker boss had to admit that he knew what he was doing.

He had been feeling really good, like he was back in control, when he called Liz for the fifth time that day.

She hadn't answered the phone at home so he had called her mobile and she told him she was at the park with Luke.

'Don't worry,' she said before he could say anything. 'No one is here. It's just me and Luke today and I'm wearing glasses and a hat.'

'Good,' he said and he felt proud of how she had kept their secret. It was a private matter and he'd hate for other people to get the wrong impression of who he was.

As they talked he could hear something in the background, something that sounded like a television, but at the time he hadn't thought much about that. He had been concentrating on apologising to Liz one more time, promising her that it would never happen again. Each time it happened he felt sure it was the last time. This time he was absolutely certain that he would never hurt her again.

She said she accepted his apology. She understood that he loved her and that sometimes he just got a little angry. She said she would see him for dinner and she asked him what he wanted her to cook. She had said she would see him for dinner but she had lied.

He had come home to find the flowers wilting on the front step. The chocolates had melted.

The wilted flowers had pissed him right off. They had been really expensive and she had just left them on the step to die. He had opened the door and kicked them inside the house, scattering petals and water all over the floor.

'Liz?' he had called, trying to keep the fury out of his voice. There was no reply and it was only then that he sensed the emptiness in the house. It was still light so he hadn't expected any lights to be on but Luke was usually stuck in front of the television when he came home at night.

He had walked through the house calling to the two of them but only stale air greeted him. He hadn't even had to check the closets to know that they were gone. He knew what a house felt like when someone moved out.

Liz had opened the door at her mother's house and just stared at him like he was some sort of monster. He could see her heart beating in her neck and he knew she was afraid but that just pissed him off more.

She didn't say anything to him. She just stood there looking pathetic and he could see that she hadn't even put ice on her eye. She didn't want it to get better. She finally had something she could parade around the neighbourhood so everyone would think he was a complete waste of space.

She was the one who started it but he was the one who had ended up apologising. How the fuck did that happen? That mother of hers had come to the door and stood with her hand on Liz's shoulder and she hadn't even said anything. All she'd done was shake her head like he was a piece of shit not worth talking to.

He had felt the rage start to build then. 'I could kill them both right now,' he'd thought, but he had swallowed his pride and left instead.

He had to go home and clean up the mess he'd made with the flowers and then he had to cook himself dinner and clean up the broken plates after he'd thrown them against the wall.

He hadn't seen Luke that night. It was the first time he hadn't put the boy to bed since he'd been born and that was just wrong. He knew he had lashed out. He understood his mistake, but he had assured her that it wouldn't happen again. He had shocked himself and that was the truth. He'd just been so angry about the chicken. He couldn't seem to control the anger. One moment he was just a little annoyed and the next moment he was in a freight train going through a tunnel and he could only stop after he had hit something.

After he had hit Liz.

He didn't start out wanting to hit her. He wished he could explain that to her so that she understood. He started every day hoping to be a better husband and a better father. He wanted to be a better man but some days it felt like the world was conspiring against him. He would be running late for work and then he wouldn't be able to find a parking spot and then he would finally get in to find he'd missed a deadline because someone had told him the wrong date and then he would cop shit from everyone else on the project. By the time the day ended all he wanted was a bit of peace. He looked forward to a clean house and a good meal and some quiet time with his wife. And then he opened the door and everything was a mess and Liz was pissed off because he was home late and she would just sit there and not say anything to him and he would get so hot he wanted to lie in a bath of ice. He would feel the heat rushing through his body, going into his hands and feet, and he would feel burned by the anger he was experiencing.

Afterwards he would always have to apologise but that was okay because afterwards he felt in control and at peace. Afterwards he could be a better man.

It wasn't like he was some loser who hit women for fun. He had never hurt a woman before Liz.

Well, there had been that silly bitch before Liz. He couldn't even remember her name now. It was Sally or Sarah, something with an S. She was a lot shorter than Liz with frizzy red hair. He had kind of liked her hair; it looked like her head was wrapped in flames. Her skin was pure white. She didn't have any freckles or anything. She was really into herself as well. She kept going on about how she could have been a supermodel if she was taller.

She hated the sun. She wouldn't even go for a walk without covering up every inch of her body. She used to talk about herself constantly, always starting sentences with, 'Well I think . . .'

143

'You think too much,' he told her once but she just thought he was being funny. She had laughed at him.

They'd had a fight over going to the beach. They had planned to meet friends at two and she was running late.

He hated running late. When he was running late he felt twisted inside. He found it hard to breathe. If someone else was running late he knew, just knew, that they were never coming, that they were lost. He could never be late because then people would think he was lost or not coming at all. He needed people to know that he would always be there.

On the day his mother left he had been the last one at school waiting to be picked up. All the other children had been greeted by their delighted mothers and he had stretched his head towards every car sound he heard, getting more and more panicked as each minute passed and his mother had still not arrived.

The school was mostly empty and the secretary kept coming out of her office to peer at him like he might actually know where his mother was. The bigger children left and some of the teachers left and the quiet began to eat away at Alex. He was only five and he couldn't help his tears. The secretary was kind. She let him sit on her lap and gave him a biscuit.

Eventually his father turned up.

Not his mother. His father.

If someone was late Alex knew it was possible that he would never see them again.

Besides, it was rude to be late.

Each minute that passed churned his insides a little more.

He had told Sally or Sarah a time half an hour before they actually needed to leave and still she wasn't ready when he came to get her and then she insisted on waiting twenty minutes just to let the sunblock absorb properly. Alex had felt the rage sneak up on him. Usually it felt like a hot explosion in his stomach that spread outwards but this time he actually thought he was doing fine and then all of a sudden he hated her so much he wanted her to die.

She had been staring at her white skin in the mirror and he had pushed her from behind. It wasn't a big push but the mirror had cracked and she had a small cut that didn't even need stitches. It wouldn't have mattered if she wasn't so obsessed with her face.

Jesus, the noise she made. It was funny when he thought about it now. Of course the relationship was over but he had never expected her brother on the doorstep.

At first Alex hadn't even understood what the guy was doing there. He didn't want to talk about what had happened at all. He had obviously just accepted his sister's version of events. If he had given Alex a chance, Alex could have told him that women twist things.

Afterwards Alex had needed stitches under his eye and he had a broken arm. Not that he could go to the police. He didn't need any questions. He told his father he fell down some stairs when he was drunk. He told the hospital the same thing and then he told one of the nurses that he'd been drinking because it was the anniversary of his mother's death. He told her how his mother had drowned in a boating accident when he was only five years old and the nurse had even cried a little. People preferred the lies.

His father had laughed at the thought of him being so drunk he fell down some stairs. 'I've done that a couple of times myself,' said Frank and then he had offered Alex a beer.

Frank liked to think of Alex as a real Aussie bloke. It was something he respected. When Alex punched someone at a university party Frank had been almost proud. Alex was small like Frank and they both hated the idea of some other bloke using his height and his strength to intimidate them. Frank didn't need to know that some seventeen-year-old had beaten him up for hurting his sister.

Alex learned his lesson after Sarah or Sally. He had practised keeping a lid on his rage and after he met Liz he thought he would never need to be angry again.

It hadn't fazed Liz that he liked things a certain way. She'd been happy to let him organise their dates and take care of things. She'd even managed to get her time issue under control. It had been so good when they first got together; he couldn't imagine ever being mad at her. But then when Luke came along it felt like she forgot about him.

Once she got all weird and told him she would give her life for Luke.

'What about me?' he had asked, but she had just laughed at him. He had wanted to hit her then. He had wanted to hit her so badly he had to sit on his hands. He managed to control it that time but he knew that it was coming.

Liz changed. She turned into someone who didn't care about him. She was either phoning him every five minutes or pretending he wasn't there. Greg at work had told him that would happen. 'They go strange for a few months, mate. Trust me. All you can do is hold on and wait for it to pass.' Alex had just smiled at Greg, amused that the man thought he could offer advice when his own marriage was in the toilet.

Alex knew Liz loved him but he should always have been the centre of her universe, and after Luke came she wasn't even interested in sex anymore. The first time he shoved her he hadn't really been trying to hurt her. Not really. He just wanted to get out of the house and away from her. He had told her he was sorry but he noticed that afterwards she tried really hard to be the kind of wife he needed. She put Luke in his room where he belonged and she got interested in sex again. He hadn't wanted to hurt her but it did seem to make things better afterwards. It really did.

He knew she was just trying to make him sorry by saying that they needed to be apart. She knew he was the best thing that had ever happened to her.

Women said it was all about you figuring out what you'd done wrong and then apologising but all they really wanted was to break your balls. He'd apologised again and again, hadn't he? He had tried to make it up to her. He had promised he would see someone to figure out how to control his temper, but what was the point of that if she wasn't going to come back to him? The shrinks were all full of crap anyway.

He'd had enough of people telling him what to do, of Liz telling him what to do. It was time to take control. Time to show Liz that he couldn't be pushed around. He would keep his kid as long as he wanted. He would keep him forever if he wanted. Yeah, he liked that idea. He would keep Luke forever. Then he would be the one holding all the cards. He would be the one who could say when she got to come over and what she got to do with him. If he told the courts what kind of a person she had become they would definitely hand custody over to him. Unless of course they believed all the lies Liz and that mother of hers told.

He liked the idea of being the one in charge of Luke.

Liz would be the one sitting at home with a broken heart trying to figure out the right words to use to make him come back and bring Luke with him. Maybe he would leave with Luke. They could leave the state or the country and start a new life somewhere. He would miss Liz but maybe that's what he had to do to make her realise how much she loved him. In his heart he knew she really loved him and she was just being difficult right now.

He needed to find a way to take control of the situation. That was the most important thing. Maybe if his father had taken control with his mother she would never have left. Women liked to feel that the man was in charge. He had to make sure that Liz understood that.

'Daddy, I'm tired now. Can we go home?'

'We'll go home in a little while, Luke—go and play some more.'

'But I'm bored. I want to go home.'

'Jesus, Luke, quit your whining or I'll . . .' Alex stopped when he saw other parents looking. Everyone was always watching. Other mothers looked to see what he would do with his kid and other fathers looked like they were glad Luke wasn't their problem.

Luke turned on the waterworks and he could feel himself getting really angry but he took a few deep breaths and said, 'Come on, mate, don't cry; come on, you're a big boy. What about a slurpee?'

'A real slurpee?'

'Yeah, a real slurpee.' Alex held on to a laugh. One minute they were covered in tears and snot and the next they were happy. Kids were fucking hilarious.

'Mum says slurpees is bad for my teeth.'

'Well Mum's not in charge today so let's go and get you one.'

''Kay.'

She was always trying to control everything. The poor kid was getting brainwashed by Liz and that mother of hers. It wasn't right for a boy to be living with two women. A boy needed a man's influence. There was no way he was going to let his son grow up in a house run by women and turn into some fag. No way was that going to happen.

He handed Luke the slurpee and watched his son's eyes widen at the cold. It was so funny that he just had to tell Liz.

He forgot about everything else and he just pushed the button. Only Liz would understand how funny Luke could be. The first time they'd given him a lick of an ice cream you would have thought the kid had seen God. He couldn't open his mouth wide enough for more. He just sat there in his stroller with his tongue hanging out hoping for another lick.

She answered on the first ring. He liked that she was waiting for his call.

'Hey, Liz,' he said, trying to keep from laughing as Luke tried to suck up a big chunk of ice.

'Alex, oh thank God. Where are you? Why haven't you brought him home?'

Alex felt his laugh dissolve. He hated it when she questioned him like this.

'Why are you getting crazy? I told you where we were.'

'Alex, it's really late now and I'm getting concerned. I need you to bring Luke home now.'

Alex didn't like her tone.

'Relax, Liz; I just called to tell you the funniest thing. You wouldn't believe how funny it is. I got Luke a slurpee and his eyes got all wide and . . .'

'You got him what? Alex, you know I don't like him to have junk food. Now he's going to be mental all night. Just bring him home, okay? Bring him home right now.'

Alex bristled at Liz's instructions.

'I'm not bringing him home now, Liz. We're having fun. Don't tell me what to do. You're really going to have to watch your tone when you talk to me. When you come home again we're going to have to have a little talk about that.'

Liz was silent on the other end of the phone but Alex could hear her breathing—fast, panting breaths like she was trying to stop the words coming out. In the background he heard her mother say, 'Don't let him push you, Liz,' and then Liz spat the words she had been trying to hold back and Alex could feel her rage push at him through the phone.

'Are you fucking kidding me? Are you completely crazy? I'm not coming home, Alex. Why can't you get that? It's like you're completely delusional. What the fuck is wrong with you? I need to stay away from you. You make me so angry. Just bring him home now. Right now!'

Alex felt a strong pain in his chest. This wasn't like Liz. What did she mean by saying that she wasn't coming home? Did she mean she wasn't coming home forever? Did she mean never?

He stood up straighter, listening to her irate panting on the phone. He wanted to feel taller because he could feel himself shrinking. She was making him small again. She was making him five.

'I don't understand, Liz. Do you mean you're never coming home . . . never?'

'Fuck yes, Alex, that's exactly what I mean. I am so sick of trying to get through to you. Bring my son home. Bring him home now, do you understand? I want him home now.'

'Why are you screaming at me, Liz? I don't understand.'

'Bring him home, Alex,' she said.

'What do you mean you're not coming home? You said you just needed time and after last night I thought . . .'

'Last night was a mistake, Alex, do you get me? It was a mistake. I have no intention of ever coming back. You know that we don't belong together. I can't have you hurt me anymore. I just can't.'

'But I need you, Liz . . . I told you that. I need you . . . you can't leave me like my mother did. You just can't.'

Alex felt his throat constrict, like he was going to cry. She couldn't be telling him the truth.

'I'm not your fucking mother, Alex. I'm so sick of hearing

about her. Bring him the fuck home or I swear I'll get the police and they will arrest you and throw you in jail.'

Alex couldn't breathe properly. This wasn't how Liz was supposed to talk to him. She had no right to threaten him and yell at him.

'I don't like anything that you're saying, Liz. I don't like the way you're talking to me,' he said very quietly and slowly so that she would understand she was pushing him.

On the other end of the phone he heard her take a deep breath.

'Look, Alex, I just need you to bring Luke home now, okay? I'm sorry I yelled but I got a little angry. Bring him home now and we'll talk.'

All she cared about was Luke. She just wanted him to bring her kid home and then get out of her life. She wanted to move on and find another man and have other kids. She wanted to erase him from her life just like his mother had done. Well there was no way he was going to let that happen.

'Alex,' said Liz, 'are you still there? Please just bring him home now . . . just bring him home.'

'No, Liz,' said Alex. 'I don't think so. I really don't think so.'

'Alex, please. He needs to be home with me. He's going to need dinner soon.'

'You're breaking my heart, Liz. Do you know that? You're breaking my heart.'

'Alex . . . you need . . .'

Nicole Trope

'I wish you knew what this felt like, Liz. I wish you knew how awful it felt to have someone hurt you like this. You should know how this feels, Liz. You need to learn how this feels. You can't do this to someone and not ever have to feel this.'

'Alex, just bring him home. Nothing else matters now. Please . . .'

But Alex didn't let her finish. He ended the call and switched off the phone again.

He sank onto the floor of the arcade.

'Whatcha doing, Dad?' said Luke.

'I'm . . . I'm just sitting, Luke—just sitting.'

'Can I sit too?'

'Yeah . . . yeah, you can sit too.'

Luke hunched down next to him and sucked at his straw, making gurgling noises as he got to the bottom of the cup.

She wasn't coming home. He couldn't believe it. He had done everything right and she still didn't love him enough to come home.

Suddenly he was so tired he wanted to sleep. He wanted to sleep forever. She wasn't coming home again, not ever.

He sat on the floor trying to work his way through the words. She wasn't ever coming home again. It was inconceivable. All these months he had known that she would soon be home again. He had known that if he could just say the right thing she would be

154

back in his bed and Luke would be back in his room. Now she had used the word 'never'.

The floor was sticky and people were walking around the two of them and staring.

Alex stood up even though his legs were shaking.

'Come on, Luke,' he said, trying to keep his voice strong. 'Let's go for a little drive.'

8

Liz dropped her head into her hands.

Alex in the anger phase swirled through her head.

Alex holding his breath.

Alex clenching his hands into fists.

Alex gathering his rage into a tight ball and nursing it until it could explode.

The image of what he looked like before he lashed out never left her mind. She preserved it for future reference after each encounter so that she would know when it was time to run.

But she never ran.

She just stood there and took what was coming to her. She understood on some level that she was sacrificing herself for her child. She knew that she could never leave the house and leave Luke trapped inside with his raging father. So she just stood there or lay there.

Now she had brought on the rage when she was not there to see the end result.

She could not bear the thought of Luke watching that rage take over his father. She prayed that they would stay in a public place. Alex hated anyone to see him out of control. He was the best man to be with in public, but Liz knew that the wider his smile in front of the world, the harder he hit behind closed doors.

How could she have been so utterly, utterly stupid? She wanted to tear at her hair and howl but her body was stilled by the shock of her actions.

'Perhaps it wasn't the best time . . .' began Ellen.

'I know,' shouted Liz. 'Don't you think I know how stupid that was? Don't you think I wish I had kept my mouth shut? I don't know what happened. I just don't know what happened.'

'You're worried,' said Ellen. 'It's understandable.'

'Isn't that what you wanted me to do, Mum? I stood up to him. And now I've made a bad situation worse.'

'I didn't want you to yell at him, Liz. I know how unpredictable he can be.'

'Actually, Mum, you have no idea at all about Alex. You don't have a fucking clue.'

'Please, Liz—there's no need for that kind of language. The police will be here soon and I'm sure we can get all of this sorted out. You told the police you were calling your father. Why don't you do that?'

'You do it.'

'He doesn't want to hear from me, Liz . . .'

'Please, Mum, could you just stop playing politics and call him?'

'I'm not the one you're angry at, Liz.'

Liz didn't reply. She stood up and went to the bathroom, where she let the tears come. She had been determined to stay detached and cool and to be strong. She was a complete joke. She wanted to laugh at herself but her body was heaving with anguish instead.

'I'm sure he's just running late,' called her mother.

Liz wished she would just shut up. She heard her mother head towards the kitchen for the fridge and the cubes of ice that made her drinking a civilised indulgence rather than a low-class problem. Liz sat on the floor of the bathroom and tried to figure out how it had come to this.

What had possessed her to yell at him?

She was not allowed to raise her voice to him.

That was one of the triggers.

She was not allowed to berate him.

That was one of the triggers.

She was not allowed to demand things of him.

That was one of the triggers.

She knew this. She knew all these things and yet she had done everything wrong.

Now she had no idea what was going to happen. No idea at all.

He could decide to drive straight over to the house and beat the crap out of her. She pictured him speeding along the roads, skidding around corners.

Please, God, don't let him have an accident with Luke in the car.

She pictured him biting his lip and muttering to himself.

Please, God, don't let him turn his anger on Luke.

She pictured him running up the front path, shouting her name, spitting his fury.

Please, God, let him come here and hit me. Let him come here and bring my boy and hit me.

But Alex was probably not on his way to the house. He knew she was here with her mother. He wouldn't risk exposing himself in that way; he would find another way to punish her. Of that she was completely sure. He wanted her to feel the same pain he was feeling, that's what he'd said.

How could she have been so stupid? When he had been holding on to hope that they would get back together he had been working hard to show her what a good father he was, what a good man he was. Now that hope was gone and there was no reason for him to be good at all. There was nothing holding him back—and she couldn't smother the fear that he was capable of a great deal more than a punch to the eye.

Liz bit her hand to stop herself from screaming.

What was he going to do?

What was he going to do?

She had read the articles just like everyone else. She sat in front of the computer shaking her head at the terrible things men did to their children to punish their ex-wives. To break their hearts. To make them feel pain.

Until now she had always been a little alarmed by her own fascination with these stories. She read every piece written on the man who threw his daughter off a bridge and chided herself for being ghoulish. Now, in a moment of clarity, she realised that her interest was not merely voyeuristic; it was more a case of forewarned is forearmed.

There were signs that each article listed. Signs a woman needed to look for—although the signs meant nothing unless you viewed them in hindsight.

Plenty of men beat their wives but did not hurt their children.

Plenty of men were controlling but did not hurt their children.

Men could be depressed and not hurt their children, and they could hurt themselves but not hurt their children.

How could you ever know if you had a husband or a boyfriend who was going to be the one?

The articles listed new boyfriends as a problem so Liz stayed away from men altogether. She barely left her mother's house at night.

The articles told of men not seeing their children enough so Liz made sure Alex saw Luke as often as he wanted.

The articles spoke of men feeling powerless and out of control so Liz made sure that Alex thought the decisions were his.

And still it was not enough for him.

What would be enough?

To Liz the most shocking thing about the man on the bridge was that he had showed no signs of being a monster. As she had scrolled through the articles she had come across a picture of the man and his ex-wife when they were still together. They were at a party of some sort, dancing. He was in a tuxedo and she was in a sea-green ruffled dress with a low back and a row of sparkles at the neck. They were laughing and embracing as they shared their joy with the camera.

All the pictures of the man since his horrifying act of revenge made him look insane. His hair was long and bushy and he stared at the camera with dead eyes, but in the picture from the party he could have been an accountant or a butcher. He could have been anyone, but now he was the man who had done this terrible thing.

Did his wife have any idea of who he would become? Was there anything she could have done to save her child?

Alex had all the signs, but having the signs didn't necessarily mean anything.

Until they meant something.

9

Liz stared at the ceiling for awhile and then she pulled her mobile phone out of her pocket and called Rhonda. She needed help to get her through this. She could call Molly—she and Molly spent a lot of time together now—but Molly wouldn't understand. Molly was busy planning her own wedding to a nice doctor who never raised his voice.

But she needed someone else here now. If she was left alone with her mother they would begin playing the blame game and Liz didn't need anyone else to tell her that she had fucked up. So she called Rhonda because Rhonda knew what it felt like to fuck up.

•

Liz sat next to Rhonda at group and sometimes when she spoke Rhonda held her hand. Rhonda's skin was dry and peeling and her nails were bitten short but her hand gave Liz the certainty that she would not be judged. At the first group meeting Liz had slunk into the room trying not to feel like a fifteen-year-old terrified of her father's reaction instead of a mother with a child of her own. She had hung back when they'd taken their seats, unsure and unwilling.

'Sit here, darl,' a thin, ropey woman who could have been her age or her mother's age said.

Liz sat down, grateful to be included without having to say anything. The woman's name was Rhonda and as it turned out she was only a couple of years older than Liz.

Rhonda sucked furiously on one cigarette after another all meeting and didn't seem to care when she dropped ash on her faded jumper. Under her eye a bruise was in the yellow stage, and her wrist was wrapped in plaster.

'Kicked him out last year, but that doesn't mean the bastard doesn't still come back every now and again,' she said without waiting for any questions from Liz.

On nights when Luke wanted his daddy and Liz wanted to kill her mother she could call Rhonda, who had walked all the same paths before her.

'You have to look at this as phase one,' said Rhonda. 'Phase one is when you get away from the dickhead and find a place to lick your wounds. That's where you are now. Don't rush it, Liz.

Wait until you've figured out a way to deal with him. Wait until all the papers are signed and maybe he's found someone else to get him through the night. Phase two is when you get your own place, get a job and start living your life without worrying about him getting around you.'

'And what's phase three?' Liz asked.

'Phase three is when you've got enough money to live your life and get your hair done and there is some lovely man warming your bed.'

Liz laughed. 'Where are you, Rhonda?'

'Well, it's been a while for me so I would say I'm in phase two—unless of course I let him talk me back into bed like I did a couple of months ago. Then I fall right back into phase one, 'cause the moment he pulls out he gives me a smack.'

'Oh, Rhonda,' Liz said.

'Yep: oh, Rhonda,' Rhonda replied.

They were so far apart in the world that they never would have met without the group. Liz had travelled a few suburbs and a good few levels of society—the levels that weren't supposed to exist in Australia—to find the group. When she'd called the number from the notice board at the shopping centre a woman on the other end had given her a choice of locations. There were meetings close to where she lived with her mother but she didn't want to go there. Imagine the horror of turning up and finding the next-door neighbour in the circle, sipping her cup of coffee and waiting to tell her own tale of woe. Instead, she found a place where she could just be Liz, and if she wanted to talk she could, but if she kept silent she would simply be the woman in group who didn't say anything. She would not have to be Elizabeth Harrow whose father made all that money and then left his wife or Liz Harrow who married that lovely polite Alex and had a little boy who went to school with our little boy.

Rhonda came from a family where getting hit by your husband was something that just happened to you. Her father hit her mother and her brother hit his wife and everyone hit the kids. As a child Rhonda had watched things go round and round and vowed she would never find herself trapped and spinning the same way. She wouldn't let anyone touch her kids, and once she figured out that her husband was as full of shit as the other husbands who said they were sorry, she kicked him out.

She and Liz had coffee after group every week and when Liz told Rhonda where she lived and who she was Rhonda hadn't even blinked. 'There's a lot like you that come every now and again. Sometimes a woman named Bethany comes. Her husband is a plastic surgeon and she drives the prettiest car you've ever seen. You wouldn't believe anyone could look so perfectly together unless they were standing in front of a camera. But once she opens her mouth she's just as sad and pathetic as the rest of us. Dress it up how you like, but a smack from a rich man hurts just as much

as a smack from a poor one. I don't care where you come from.
We're all in the same place right now, aren't we?'

•

In the bathroom Liz was staring at her mobile phone. She pressed her fingers over the buttons the way Luke did.

'Click clack, Mum. Did you hear dem go click clack?'

'I'll be there as soon as,' Rhonda had said. She hadn't even asked any questions.

Rhonda was coming and maybe she would have something different to say and give Liz something different to think about.

•

'You were right to call the police but I know it's all going to blow over,' called Ellen from the kitchen. She didn't even know if Liz could hear her but she had to keep talking.

'I think it will be fine, I think . . .' but Ellen didn't know what to think anymore. She sipped at her whisky, letting it burn its way slowly down her throat. She wanted to find the right words to comfort Liz but every time she opened her mouth she messed up.

She was still waiting to get to the part where she had all the answers. As a child the magic of the teenage years promised clarity and control and then her twenties beckoned with freedom and her own decisions.

She thought when she married Jack and he seemed to be doing so well that she had achieved the holy grail of existence. She was in love and she was married and there was enough money for the bills. Life was under control. She wanted a baby and she had managed pregnancy without a hitch and then of course it had all fallen apart in her thirties. She wasn't sure when she had discovered that Jack had stopped talking to her, touching her or even wanting to be in the same room with her. When Liz was born she had been so absorbed by the baby that she hadn't noticed, not really. You could sit around and discuss it all you liked but the truth was that no one was really sure when a marriage started to die. It could have been the one big moment when he confessed his adultery but it could also have been a thousand little moments when she missed what he was trying to say and he missed what she was trying to do.

It could have been too much television and too little sex or it could have been the towels on the bathroom floor and a forgotten anniversary. Even now Ellen couldn't pinpoint the moment that the wall of their marriage started to chip away. Perhaps it was the responsibility of parenthood or maybe it was because they had little to discuss after, 'How was your day?'

Ellen had no idea what happened and then the more he ignored her the more she clamoured for his attention and Jack had hated that. She had felt like a small child asking to be picked up.

She had never, for one moment, imagined he would find someone else—especially not someone like Lilly. She was so round. She oozed out of tight skirts and giggled behind her hands like a child. How could she be the right woman for Jack?

Alex was wrong from the day Liz met him. He was too small, too contained and then when he opened his mouth to speak she knew that he was still more child than man. Well, most of them were, weren't they?

Alex wanted to play happy families but he had no idea that there were always going to be times when things got difficult. Ellen had sensed this but there was no point in trying to convince Liz of anything. They had reached that stage where everything she said was met with a contemptuous snort from her daughter. It was fair enough. She remembered being the same way with her mother. But Liz's responses had an edge to them, something razor sharp that spoke of Ellen's failures as a mother.

She had seen Alex as the wrong man for her daughter but at most she'd seen a strained existence similar to her own followed by a divorce. Alex was so small compared to Liz, there was no way she could have predicted that he could possibly hurt her so much.

And now here they were. She couldn't find the right words to comfort her daughter because she couldn't find those words for herself.

It could be nothing. Alex could walk through the door and there could be some shouting and screaming and then it could all just go back to the way it had been. Or—and the 'or' made Ellen take another sip of her drink—or they could find themselves in the middle of some front-page news story. They could become that family, that mother, that grandmother.

People got in their cars to make a quick trip to the shops and never came back. People went in for routine tests and received a death sentence. Things could change in an instant.

Ellen shook her head. It was all going to be fine. She couldn't think of it any other way. Where would Alex take Luke anyway?

He couldn't get on a plane to another country but he might leave the state.

Who would she and Liz be without Luke? How would they be? If Alex disappeared into the middle of Australia with Luke how would she and Liz survive?

Luke had been the way back for them. He had forced Liz into a place where she needed the lifeline of a mother, even a mother as flawed as Ellen.

She was pleased that the police were coming although it did seem to be a bit of an overreaction. Didn't the police have better things to do? She looked into her empty glass and thought about pouring herself another drink, but it would not look good to have the police arrive and find her slowly on her way to oblivion. She filled the kettle instead. After this afternoon was over she would fill her glass to the brim and sleep off the afternoon in a dreamless rest.

And then after a few weeks it was probably time to tell Liz that she needed a place of her own. She loved having Luke in the house but sometimes Liz made her feel the same way Jack used to. They both looked at her like she was clueless. Perhaps she was clueless? Ever since the day Jack left she had been a spider hanging on to a thin line of web swinging in the wind. It was inevitable that the web would break, inevitable that she would find herself free falling with no hope of being saved. Was this the day then? Was today the day when her whole world fell apart in a way that couldn't be rosily viewed through a whisky glass?

Ellen opened the bottle and poured herself just half a tot more. She would think positive thoughts instead. Alex would walk through the door any minute now and they would all get a stern lecture from the police about wasting their valuable time.

She would call Jack now and get him to come over and maybe they could discuss him buying a place for Liz and Luke. Heaven knows the man had enough money.

•

Rhonda arrived ten minutes later. 'I was at the big shopping centre. My ex's got the kids. I thought I'd give myself a treat. I called Rebecca. Hope you don't mind.'

Liz shook her head. She didn't mind. Right now she would tell the whole world if she thought it would get Luke home.

'How long have they been missing?' asked Rebecca when she arrived.

'Over an hour now,' said Liz.

No one said, 'It's only an hour—what are you worrying about?' or 'Are you completely crazy to be dragging us away from our lives when he's only an hour late?'

No one said that.

'I suppose he's not answering his phone,' said Rhonda, talking more to herself than anyone else.

Liz shook her head and ran her hand across her face, catching a stray tear she thought she had finished with in the bathroom.

'I'm really scared for Luke,' said Liz.

'What a fucken wanker,' said Rhonda.

'Have you called the police?' Rebecca asked.

Liz nodded, not trusting herself to speak. She was getting impatient with the questions. The answers were obvious and she felt a slight twinge of regret that she had called the women from the group. They looked incongruous standing in her mother's pale living room. Her mother was standing off to the side holding her face in a silent smile. She had not been pleased when Liz told her Rhonda and Rebecca were coming.

'What on earth for, Liz?' Ellen had asked. 'This will all be over soon. Alex won't like coming back to a house full of people. You know that.'

'I do, Mum,' said Liz, 'but I need them here. I can't explain it. I guess it's because they understand what someone like Alex can be like. I'd rather they were here when he got back anyway. I don't need him starting any crap with me today.'

'I understand, Liz. You keep sidelining me but I do understand. I've watched you and Alex these past few months and I know what he's like.'

'God, Mum, it's not a judgement call, okay? I'm not saying they're better to have around than you are. I just want a bit of extra . . . I don't know: support, I guess.'

'Well, your father's coming now as well. He wasn't happy about leaving his precious football game but I didn't give him much choice.'

Liz hadn't had anything to say to that so she had made her way to the living room to look out of the window in the hope of seeing Alex's car turn the corner.

Liz watched now as Rhonda, Rebecca and her mother made awkward conversation. She knew she could help things along—Rebecca liked gardening and so did her mother, and Rhonda was addicted to the same television shows as Ellen—but Liz couldn't muster the energy for anything other than worry.

'Well,' said Rebecca, 'I guess we'll just have to wait. I'm sure it's all going to be fine. He's not the first man to do something like this. Not the first man at all. It's ego and pride, you know.

He just wants to let you know he's in control. He'll bring him back soon enough.'

Rebecca had never had children with her first husband. Liz bit her lip, trying not to be irritated by Rebecca's positive attitude.

•

Rebecca had breezed in to that first meeting on the dot of ten in a dress lush with flowers. Her hair was pulled back with a band and her clear skin and glowing eyes lit up the room. Just about every woman in the group hated her on sight. She had only just taken over running the group and she chirped away about setting boundaries and being strong and powerful. She was into positive affirmations and treating yourself with respect. It was a couple of months before Rebecca's story came out and afterwards Liz was sorry for laughing at her. Sorry for judging her as uptight and full of shit.

One week they had a self defence lesson.

The man who came in to play the offender was padded up from head to toe.

'I wonder where I can get one of those,' Liz said mostly to herself.

'Just look at you speaking and making a joke,' said Rhonda.

'Now ladies, please. We need to pay attention so we can learn the sensitive areas on the body.'

'I know all about those,' said Cherry.

'This will help you all. This will allow you to feel a little more in control,' said Rebecca.

'Yeah and then I can beat the crap outa him,' snorted Glenda.

'That's not what this is about, Glenda,' said Rebecca sternly. 'This is to buy you time so you can get hold of the police or remove yourself from the situation.'

'That'll really fucking help,' said Esther, whose husband was a retired police officer.

'Most police officers will be very helpful, Esther. You have to trust the authorities to do their job.'

It was Rhonda who had snapped. 'You know what pisses us all off, Bec?' Rhonda had said, ignoring Rebecca's obvious distaste at being called 'Bec'.

'What would that be, Rhonda?'

'It's the way you sit there with your big fucken diamond ring and the picture of your three delightful kids and tell us how to figure our way out of these fucked-up relationships, when clearly your pretty skin has never, ever been marked by someone's fist.'

Rebecca had looked at Rhonda for a long minute, and then at all the other woman assembled in the circle. Then she had taken a picture out of her bag and passed it around.

It was a picture of Rebecca in a hospital. There were tubes in her arms and her leg was in a splint. Her nose looked like it had been broken and on one side of her head a whole chunk of hair was missing. Both eyes were plums, shining on her face.

No one had said anything after that and they had moved onto words that had power.

Later at coffee time Liz had come back from the bathroom to find Rebecca and Rhonda huddled in a corner. Rhonda who looked like she never shed a tear was crying and Rebecca was saying, 'It's okay Rhonda. Now you know it's possible to move on. This does not have to define the rest of your life. It doesn't have to be who you are five years from now.'

•

Rhonda took charge and made tea and coffee for everyone.

'I can feel it's not right,' said Liz, taking a mug of coffee from Rhonda.

Rhonda nodded. Rebecca was big on you trusting your feelings.

'If you can see him working his way up to something,' Rebecca always said, 'get out. Trust your feelings and make an excuse to get away from him if you're still with him or get him to leave if you're living apart. Trust your instincts. That's what you can count on.'

Liz's instincts told her she had fanned the flames of Alex's resentment. She hadn't just touched it or added a few sticks; she had poured a whole can of petrol on it.

The doorbell rang; it was Liz's father.

'It's turned into a fucking tea party,' thought Liz.

'What did you call me for?' asked Jack, looking around the room.

'I told you why, Jack,' said Ellen. 'They don't send police out if they think you're just being a hysterical woman. The police are coming and Liz wanted you to be here. When Alex does bring him home maybe you and he could have a little chat.'

Her father nodded and sat down to wait.

Liz said nothing. She was just grateful that her mother seemed certain that Luke was coming home. Liz wished she could be so sure herself.

One hour and twenty-five minutes late

The house was a single storey on one of those 'quiet' streets everyone always wanted to buy in. It had the clean look of constant upkeep but it didn't scream money.

The pitched roof was painted slate grey. In front of the house was a garden where the winter flowers were beginning to show themselves. There were patches that Robert would bet contained all the beauty that would arrive in spring. The lawn was trimmed and the flowerbeds even. The garden was loved in the obvious way that you sometimes saw in houses where older people lived. People who had the time and the patience to wait for the reward of a garden.

This was not the garden of a recently single woman. Robert would bet that this was the house Liz Harrow had grown up in.

It was one of those suburbs where the old folks on a pension lived next door to the young folks who knocked everything down and threw up a McMansion that covered every square inch of ground. Once it may even have had more of those pensioners struggling to get through the month but the whole of Sydney was gentrifying itself, one suburb at a time.

Robert and Dave got out of the car and looked around. They'd been on the street for about two minutes but not one car had driven past them. Robert had hoped their visit might coincide with the arrival of the father and then they could give him a bit of a shock and maybe stop him from being such a prick in the future. 'No such luck,' he said softly.

'What?' said Dave.

Robert shook his head. 'I wanted the guy to turn up now and then we could . . .'

'Yeah, I know,' said Dave. 'It would have been my pleasure to scare the shit out of him.'

Robert grunted in reply. Dave had a thing about men who hit their wives. He never explained it but Robert knew there was a long story behind his distaste for violent men. He wanted to remind Dave that they had no real idea of the truth. It could be that the man had never lifted his hand to his wife.

Robert looked at the gleaming house across the street. The man in the garden had stopped mowing his lawn to stare at them. The police were obviously not regular visitors in this neighbourhood. Robert waved and the man lifted his hand a little but he didn't start the mower again. Robert debated going over the road to say something but then let that idea go. Right now they were only here to keep a member of the public happy. Right now nothing illegal was going on and there was no reason to talk to the neighbours.

He and Natalie had always wanted to build the big house with a swimming pool but had decided that they didn't want to build it with each other before the plans even got through council.

Robert had loved the house he used to live in before Natalie scraped together enough to buy him out of his half. He had mowed the lawn on Sunday and painted the fence in the holidays and now some stud named Eric was living there with Natalie and his children. He had been so pissed when Eric moved in even though he could see that the man wasn't half bad. He was one of those timid little accountant types whose clothes were always clean. So not exactly a stud but he must have had something because Natalie was talking about marriage now.

Mark loved him because he was a model-train enthusiast. Natalie had let him turn the small study that had belonged to Robert into a whole town filled with trains and miniature people.

Robert made fun of the guy over a few beers but really he was grateful that he was good to the kids and he seemed to make Natalie happy. It wasn't that he was pleased about his ex-wife moving on, just that he couldn't quite kill every feeling he had for her. He wanted her to be happy.

'Looks like a nice place,' said Dave, bringing Robert back to the present, back to where he was right now. Meaning it was not a suburb where husbands and wives typically involved the police in their divorce issues. If there had actually been domestic violence in the marriage, he would bet it was kept quiet.

'Yeah,' agreed Robert.

There were a few cars parked outside the house and Robert wondered if they were for other houses or if the woman had called everyone she knew.

If she had called everyone that meant she was circling the wagons. It wasn't a good sign. If she was doing that this wasn't an ordinary case of some wanker who wanted to keep the kid until the ex was crazy. If the wagons were being circled then this was something entirely different.

There could be a lot more going on here than the woman had told Lisa.

Robert felt his gut twist a little. Maybe there was a history of violence. Maybe there was a real danger here.

They didn't even get to ring the bell before the door opened. Robert stepped into the living room to find it filled with people.

'Shit,' he thought. 'They're really worried.'

Robert took in the cream carpet and lush cream sofas and confirmed his notion that this house did not belong to the mother of the missing child. There was a marble fireplace in which a low fire was burning. Next to the fireplace was an antique wooden trolley set up with bottles of different types of whisky and glasses. Someone liked a drink.

Behind the sofa, almost hidden from view, was a toy box filled with trucks and cars and what looked like a plastic tool set. Robert wondered how long the woman had lived with her mother and whether or not they got along. It didn't matter really, but in a worst-case scenario everything eventually became relevant.

'I'm Senior Constable Robert Williams and this is Senior Constable David Mathieson—we're looking for Elizabeth Harrow,' he said.

The room was quiet with everyone taking in the idea that the police were actually here. The air was thick with tension and worry.

'That's me,' said a woman, standing up. Robert had guessed it was her already. She had been sitting in a recliner with her hands on her knees, looking into a place only she could see. There were two women sitting by her feet like handmaidens. Elizabeth Harrow was tall, taller than Robert but not taller than Dave, whose skinny noodle body towered over everyone. She was pretty, too, and he could see that once, maybe a few kilos less and a shitty husband ago, she would have been close to beautiful.

He looked over at Dave and could instantly see his partner's eyes glaze over a little. Dave liked women who were close to his size. It was a pity this wasn't a bar so they could all have a drink.

'Call me Liz, please,' she said.

'I'm Ellen Searle, Liz's mother—Luke's grandmother,' said another woman coming in from the kitchen. She listed her titles as if to make sure they knew where to place her in this family drama.

She was much smaller than her daughter and had some extra lines around her mouth and a worn look that her nice clothes and good make-up couldn't quite hide. Robert decided she was the one who liked a drink or two. When she shook hands with him he caught the sharp sweet smell of whisky floating around her like perfume.

One of the women on the floor looked familiar. She nodded at him and it took him a moment to place her before realising that she ran a domestic violence group.

So there was the answer. It explained a whole lot that she was here.

She had once come to give everyone at the station a talk on domestic violence. The staff sergeant thought they all needed a personal perspective on things. She had come on a Monday when one or two of the boys were nursing hangovers from a wedding the night before. No one had exactly made her welcome but she didn't seem bothered by their bland faces and heaved sighs. Even the women didn't seem interested in hearing about something they dealt with every day.

She looked like some Stepford wife but the first thing she had done at the talk was pin up a whole lot of pictures of her bruised body. 'These are just a few of the photos I have from five years of abuse,' she had said. The words were a simple fact and she threw them out without any obvious self-pity. In some of the pictures she was half naked but she didn't seem to care. There were broken bones and scratches and even some knife wounds. Bruises ranged from black to yellow and no part of her was left untouched. When she'd pinned up the last picture she turned around and smiled at them. Some of the young boys sat up straight after that. Robert admired her courage—she certainly made her point.

There was only one man in the room and he stood up now and held out his hand to Robert. He was obviously the grandfather. He was even bigger than his daughter. He looked Dave in the eye. Robert wondered if he knew there was a history of violence in his daughter's marriage and, if he did know, why he hadn't stopped it. His handshake was rough and strong. This was a man who worked with his hands. He could surely have done something—not that Robert would condone it, but if some man was mistreating his daughter he would have a hard time just being a cop.

The man took up too much space in the cream-coloured living room. It was possible he didn't live here at all.

'I'm Jack—Liz's dad. I was just waiting for you. I think I'll go and take a drive around the place. I've asked some of my boys to visit a few shopping centres. We'll see if we can find them.'

'Sorry,' said Robert. 'Your boys?'

The man looked down at him and took a deep breath. Robert could see he wasn't a talker but the way the women were looking at him he didn't seem to be a hitter either, despite his size. Big men with anger issues could be really dangerous, but then so could small men with ego issues. He wondered how big the man who wouldn't bring his kid home was. Robert would guess small, even though that probably wouldn't fit with this family; he would guess small.

'Sorry. I move pianos. I've got a few trucks and a few workers. They live all over so I've asked them to take a look around the centres where they live. I'm going to go up to the nearest centre to us and have a look too,' said Jack

'Can I caution you, Mr Searle, not to engage with Mr Harrow if he seems upset or if it may put the child at risk?'

'I'm not stupid,' said Jack Searle.

'Of course not,' said Dave, 'but perhaps you could leave this to the police.' Robert could hear a change in Dave's voice. Clearly he had also felt the anxiety here in this room.

'Luke is my grandson,' said Jack.

'I know, sir, but we don't want the situation to get out of hand,' said Robert.

Ellen handed Robert a picture of the father and son. She had been standing quietly holding the picture in her hands. Robert glanced down. Just as he thought: the man was small.

'I'll take that,' said Dave.

'He likes to ride in the truck,' said Jack and Robert turned to find him still standing at the door.

'I bet he does,' said Robert, remembering Mark as a three-year-old, fascinated by anything with an engine.

'I've got a proper seat for him and everything,' said Jack, staring at Robert as if defying him to question his grandparenting abilities.

'My little boy used to love that sort of thing too,' said Robert.

'So you know,' said Jack.

'I do,' nodded Robert.

Jack tipped his head just a little and Robert could see that he had been deemed fit enough to help.

'But perhaps it would be better if you remained at the house, sir.'

'Would you?' said Jack.

'No,' Robert acknowledged. 'But I am with the police.'

'I bet you're a father before you're a cop,' said Jack, glancing at his daughter, who had returned to her chair.

Robert had nothing to reply to that and Jack turned and went out of the door. Robert knew he couldn't have stopped him without using physical force. It was easier to just let the man go, and anyway, Alex Harrow could be anywhere. It was unlikely the grandfather would find him.

10

When the police introduced themselves Liz had thrown Rhonda a quick look.

Rhonda didn't believe the police could do much until you were already bleeding.

'You have to trust the authorities,' Rebecca always said.

'As far as I can tell the only person I can really trust is me,' Rhonda would always reply.

Liz didn't know what the answer was. She had never called for help. Now that was just one more thing to blame herself for.

Maybe the police wouldn't have helped, maybe Alex would have only ever spent a few hours in jail, but at least they would have known who he was. When she had called them after he was twenty minutes late she would have been able to tell them to look him up on the computer. She wouldn't have had to explain herself. She could see the policemen looking at her now and trying to figure out whether or not to trust her version of the events.

'Perhaps it would be best if we just speak to Mrs Harrow for now,' said Senior Constable Williams. His voice was even and calm, letting the jumpers on the ledge know he was there to catch them. 'Or maybe Dave can speak to your mother here and you and I can go somewhere else to talk. I think the more we know the better our chance of finding your son.'

Liz noticed her mouth was dry. She would have been happier if they'd called her neurotic and put the phone down on her.

'You need to tell me everything,' said the detective when they were seated at the dining-room table with the door slightly ajar. 'I'm going to ask you some questions and I need you to answer them honestly, okay?'

Liz nodded. 'Constable . . .' began Liz.

'Call me Robert.'

Liz thought that he looked like a Robert. He was tall, though not as tall as his partner, and he had the kind of body that had once played rugby and now drank a little too much beer. Liz looked into his caramel eyes and wondered if he really felt her pain or if he was just very good at making it seem so.

'Robert, do you think he's going to do anything to . . . to Luke . . . to my little boy?'

She had already asked the question of Rhonda and Rebecca and her mother and father. She had asked the question of herself first and then, to retain her sanity, she had sought a different answer from those around her.

'Liz, let's start with some questions and then we can figure out where to go from there. You know that legally your ex-husband doesn't have to bring your son back at a set time?'

'I know. We don't have a formal agreement yet.'

'Okay, so has Mr Harrow ever had any dealings with the police?'

'No, not that I know of.'

'Does he have a history of violence?'

Liz looked down at the rose-embroidered tablecloth. 'Yes. Yes he does.'

'So he's violent with you? Or he was before you separated?'

Violent was a strange word. It sounded like violet, which was such a pretty colour. Sometimes a bruise would go from black to violet if the right amount of blood vessels had been burst. It was such a pretty colour.

'Yeah,' she sighed, feeling her years pile up on her. 'I mean yes, he can be. I left him five months ago. I left him because he gets so angry. He has these rages and then he hurts me. I don't think he means to; I mean, I don't think he wants to. He just . . . I don't know—he just does.'

'Have you ever called the police about it? Or spoken to anyone else?'

Liz shook her head. 'Not when we were married. Now I'm part of this group and we discuss things, but while we were together I just . . . I just kept hoping it would get better.'

Robert nodded like he understood and Liz wondered how many women had told him the same thing.

'Do you think he could hurt your son?'

'I didn't think so, not until today—but today . . .'

'Today?'

'Today he's angry. I made him angry and now I don't know what he'll do. I just don't know.'

'How did you make him angry?'

'I wouldn't discuss getting back together. I don't want to go back to him and just now, when we were waiting for you, I yelled at him—and I know I shouldn't have yelled at him.'

'So he has been in contact with you?'

'Yes, but now he's switched off his phone and he wouldn't tell me where they were.'

'Has he ever hurt your son before?'

'No, never—I wouldn't have let him . . . I would never have stayed so long if Luke was in any danger.'

'Okay, does Mr Harrow use any drugs?'

'No, not that I've ever seen.'

'What about alcohol?'

'No . . . I mean he likes to have a beer but not in a big way. I don't know about before we got married.'

Liz felt the weight of all the things she didn't know about Alex holding her down. She had no idea what the truth about him was.

'Does Mr Harrow have access to any weapons of any sort?'

'You mean like guns?'

'Yes.'

'No.'

'Is he taking any medication that was given to him by a doctor or psychiatrist?'

'No—at least, I don't think so. We've been separated for five months. I've tried not to talk to him. I've tried to keep my distance.'

'Do you think he might try to leave the country?'

'Leave the country? No . . . Luke doesn't have a passport. He would need a passport to leave the country, wouldn't he?'

'Yes he would, so that's one concern out of the way. But could he try to leave the state? Does he have family anywhere else in Australia?'

'I guess he has an uncle down in Melbourne, but they're not close at all. His mother left when he was very young so they don't see much of her side of the family. I have no idea where he would go. I don't think he'd take him out of the state, I mean he's a good dad—he's usually a good dad—and he knows . . .'

'Even now I am defending him,' thought Liz.

'Is he employed?'

'Yes, he's an engineer. He works for ASPC—you know, the big company. He's got quite an important job, I think . . . at least that's what he says.'

The answers tumbled out of her mouth but Liz realised, as she spoke, that she had no idea what was real. She didn't even know if Alex still had the same job. He said he did, but he said he loved her and didn't want to hurt her. He said he would bring Luke back by two and it was past three. He said a lot of things.

'Does he have any friends with children, anyone who is also separated and may understand how he's feeling?'

'I don't think so. He has friends but most of them are still single. Alex wanted to have kids when we were still young enough to enjoy them. Most of his friends are still trying to find the right girl.'

'Is Mr Harrow a member of any gangs or anything like that?'

Liz almost giggled imagining Alex in a motorcycle gang, but she just shook her head. Where were all these stupid questions getting them? What difference did any of it make?

'Maybe you should start looking for them,' she said to Robert quietly.

'Look, Liz, nothing you've told me gives me much reason for worry. If he's never hurt your son before he's unlikely to do so now. He may just be having some extra time with the boy and, well, he may just be trying to upset you. A lot of guys pull this kind of stunt to punish their ex-wives. He's just showing you he'll do whatever he wants to do. I know what a three-year-old can be like. They'll be back as soon as your son gets a little whiney.'

Liz looked at the policeman and gifted him a small smile. 'Silly man,' she wanted to say. 'Silly, silly man.'

She tried to explain instead. Perhaps he would understand what each passing minute meant if she explained.

'I know that's what everyone says he's doing. I know that, but I also know that he's always on time. Time is very important to him. Time and order and control. He has never been late before.'

'Divorce can be difficult. It can change a person.'

Liz couldn't figure out how to make him understand. She could see him putting a tick next to her name. Tick—one more neurotic woman to waste my time. She had wanted to be dismissed as neurotic but she could see now, could feel now, that if she didn't get through to the police they would walk away without helping her. Robert already looked like he was ready to move on to the next thing. She could see his eyes shift from her face to the room and out to the lounge room where his partner was drinking a cup of tea and charming the women around him.

'He told me my time was up.'

'Your time was up? What does that mean?'

'He wants me to come back to him and last night we . . . he came over and we kind of got close and so he thought we were getting back together and he wanted me to tell him that I'd come home. But I can't tell him that because he won't get help and he won't change—I can never go back to him. I don't want to lie: I fucked up last night and now I don't want to make it worse by lying. On the phone just before I called the police again he told me my time was up. And what I'm worried about, what I'm really wondering, is what will happen now?'

Liz was crying again but there was nothing she could do about it. He stomach rolled and her head throbbed.

In her head the last conversation she had with Alex played on a nasty loop. She had yelled at him. She hadn't yelled at Alex for years. When she was living with him she had known what would happen if she yelled at him, but today her anger and her fear had burst out of her mouth and she had yelled.

Robert looked at her with his kind eyes and she knew he was getting ready to leave. He had checked the situation out and done his job. Liz could see that he would be able to go back to the station and tell everyone that she was just another woman getting hysterical over nothing.

She didn't know how to explain things so that he would understand. She was terrified that the policemen would walk out of the house and do nothing.

She could see the night come and the hours pass and she knew that if she did not have the help of the whole state she would watch the sun rise in the morning without having seen her son. She needed them to start looking for Alex and Luke, but in order to get them to do that she would have to let the police officer know that she had crossed a line. She had to admit her own stupidity. She had to accept her own culpability. Alex and Luke would have just been home late until she had ended Alex's fantasy of his perfect family existing again.

She didn't want to admit her part in it. She didn't want him to know how stupid she had been but she knew that there was no point in keeping quiet about anything now.

'I yelled at him,' she said.

'So you said.' He shrugged. 'You were probably upset.'

'In the last call we had. He called again after I called the police. I got angry at him for giving Luke a slurpee and for being late and I yelled at him and told him I was never going to go back to him. I used the word "never" and I yelled really loud and the last time I yelled at him—which was before I left him—he poured his hot coffee over me.'

Now Liz pulled her skirt up almost to her underwear and showed Robert the burn.

'You don't understand,' she said. 'I'm not allowed to yell at him.'

Robert closed his eyes and rubbed his face.

'I don't think you understand,' Liz repeated.

'Then help me understand, Liz. I don't want to push you but right now the guy has done nothing wrong—not today, at least.'

Liz tried to get the words into line. She needed to make sense.

'I left Alex five months ago after he gave me a black eye. I came here to my mother's house and since then he has tried to call me or see me every day. I haven't taken his calls and I try to see him as little as possible but every time he does get to speak to me he begs me to come back. Literally begs me.

'I have managed to keep away from him for months. But last night he came over to see Luke and we . . . we had sex and he thought it meant that we were on our way back. On the phone just now I told him we were never getting back together again. I was really angry with him and I kind of . . . I kind of snapped.'

'What did he say when you told him you were never getting back together again?'

'He said, "You're breaking my heart, Liz." And then he told me—he told me that I needed to feel as much pain as he was feeling. And then he switched off his phone.'

Robert sat back in his chair. 'Okay,' he said. 'So let's start again. Tell me everything.'

So she told him about the charming Alex and the controlling Alex and the lying Alex and the Alex who hurt her. She listed the jealous Alex and the needy Alex and the Alex who threatened her. She talked and talked and her throat dried out but she kept going until she had painted a proper picture. Until Robert knew what he was up against.

'I'll make a few calls,' said Robert when Liz had run out of words, and he got up and left the dining room, leaving Liz to wipe away her tears, trying not to picture what might happen now that her time was up, now that Alex had decided she should feel the same pain he did.

'If you left me I would die,' he had told her one night after too much wine and too little sleep.

'I will never leave you,' she had said, because she was in love and who can ever imagine being out of love?

She had watched it happen with her parents but, like everyone who had ever felt that sensational rush of emotion, she had thought, 'Not me. I will never be like that. We will never be like that.'

And now here she was and it was hard for her to believe but she wished that Alex had left her like her father had left her mother. A man's disdain could break your heart but it couldn't break your bones. A man's disdain could alienate his daughter but an angry fist could hurt a son. An angry fist could kill a little boy.

Liz rested her head on the pretty tablecloth in the dining room.

If Alex knew there was no chance he would ever get her back she could see that he would decide to hate her instead. He would hate her to protect himself. And once he hated her, was there anything he would not do to hurt her?

Liz thought not. There was nothing he wouldn't do and no line he wouldn't cross.

Her tears dripped onto the tablecloth and she closed her eyes and prayed, because what else could she do?

11

Alex switched on the phone. He could see that while it had been switched off she had been trying again and again and again. 'That's what happens,' he thought. 'I tried to tell you but you wouldn't listen and now I won't listen either. That's what happens when you won't listen.'

A stray thought floated around inside his head: 'Watch what's going to happen now.'

He wanted to laugh at the thought of her frustration but he couldn't even muster a smile. His body was weighed down by his unhappiness. He was underwater and it was hard to move. It was hard to breathe. The ache was there to stay. One day he would be an old man and the ache would still be there and with every breath he took he would know that she was gone.

He wanted to tell someone how he felt but the only person he wanted to tell was Liz. It was difficult to feel this way about her. He loved her so much he couldn't tolerate it when he hated her.

She was his best friend. She *had* been his best friend, but now . . . what was she now? She was so angry with him and he knew why, he understood why, but what he couldn't grasp was why she didn't see that she could change the whole thing. With just a few words she could put their family back together and make them both happy again. His anger and his desolation would disappear. He could be the man she wanted him to be and she would be happy again too. If she would just give him the chance to be a better husband he knew he could do it.

He would cook for the two of them. He would make the fillet steak with Béarnaise sauce she loved so much. He would sauté the asparagus and steam the baby potatoes and they could open a bottle of red wine and toast their lives and their child. He would do it if she let him. This morning, before he had picked up Luke, he had gone to the grocery store and bought all the ingredients he would need for her welcome-home dinner.

He had cleaned the house and remade Luke's bed so that the sheets would be fresh for him. He had fixed the broken latch on the front gate and put a bunch of flowers in the hall. He had seen how it would be—but it was all over now.

There was too much food for just one person in the fridge. There was too much space for just one person in the house.

He couldn't go home to the empty house. He couldn't just drop Luke off and sit alone in the silence of his home.

Liz had always known he had a temper. He had never concealed that from her. If you love someone who has a temper you learn to give them space when they need it. That's what he had done with his father. He had always been aware of what his father was feeling.

Some mornings he would walk into the kitchen and look at his dad and he would know instantly that it was not going to be a good day. On those mornings he was the invisible kid. He would open drawers and cupboards slowly, trying not to watch the moving hands looking for something to break or smash. He would take his breakfast to his room and read comics or build Lego and later read car magazines and listen to music playing so softly he had to press his ear to a speaker to hear anything. His sanctuary was always filled with things for him to do.

On very bad days he quietly slid the lock on his bedroom door, holding his breath. The lock had been broken many times, but on good days his father would help him fix it. Alex knew that there were days when Frank looked at him and didn't see his son; he saw the woman who had left him. Was it any wonder, then, that he took his anger out on Alex?

Alex had moved on from that a long time ago. He had told Liz some of the stuff but not all of it. It was something between him and his dad and they got along all right now. Barbara helped.

On good days his father understood the need for the lock. He would mumble an apology and Alex would know that he was really sorry. That was an important part of loving someone. Forgiveness was the ultimate act of love.

After a few hours or maybe even a whole day his father would come and find him and suggest going out for a burger and then Alex knew that he was okay again.

How come Liz couldn't do the same thing?

He was a human being and everyone had bad days. But she wanted to talk and she pushed and she needled and she did things he didn't like and sometimes he could see that she was pleased when he exploded, pleased when he lashed out and hurt her. She cried afterwards, of course, but in the moment, that one moment before it all went wrong, he could see that she wanted him to hit her. They didn't put that up on the internet. No one wrote articles about it either.

She wanted him to get help from some shrink but he'd tried that once at university and it was all just a load of crap. All the woman wanted him to do was talk about his mother.

'I can't remember her,' he had said.

'You just think you don't,' said the shrink, 'but you were five when she left. You must have a lot of memories of her. Maybe you just don't want to remember her.'

He had stood up then, ready to leave. The woman was pushy

and demanding. His father told him to stay away from the pushy ones.

'We still have half an hour left today,' said the shrink.

'I don't want to talk about my mother.'

'It's not really a matter of wanting,' she said, giving him a small smile with her thin lips. 'You need to discuss her because her leaving has probably had the greatest effect on your emotional development. You talk about getting angry all the time and I think it's possible that emotionally you haven't fully moved on from being five and feeling abandoned by your mother.'

Alex hadn't stayed to hear any more crap.

'Cunt,' he had whispered on his way out the door.

'What? What did you say?' she had screeched, but by the time she got out of her chair he was long gone.

He really couldn't remember his mother. He knew what she looked like now but he couldn't remember who she had been when he was five. Sometimes he dreamed of a woman with hair that matched his. It hung down her back and flashed gold in the sun. He saw her smile and he knew that she liked to wear a blue dress with red piping. Mostly what he remembered was the way she smelled. In cake shops the smell of vanilla always brought her back to him.

She had always been cooking or baking something. He had imagined she actually lived in the kitchen. When she had first left he had begged his father to buy him cake, any kind of cake.

He would take his piece and inhale the fragrance that reminded him of her. Now the smell made him sick. If Liz had wanted to bake he would tell her to go to her mother's house.

How could you say something about a person when all you had left was the smell of vanilla?

The phone showed twenty-seven missed calls. Liz was a dog with a bone. If she could just learn to let go sometimes they would all be better off. Still, it was good that she was worried about him, about them. It was good to be able to finally be the one not answering calls. Served her right.

She told him that she wasn't coming back, not ever, but he knew she was just angry. The ache in his heart wanted him to admit that she was serious but he couldn't imagine the possibility of living his life without Liz. She was just trying to get at him because she was angry about Luke being out so late and because she was probably angry at herself about last night.

She was the one who needed a shrink. She was the one who loved him and then hated him and then loved him again. He wasn't like that. He knew that he loved her with all his heart and all his soul and he only hated her when she pushed him and when she told lies.

Liz liked to lie. He hadn't known that about her until the day she left.

In the last five months all he had been handed were a whole lot of lies. He knew that she was always at the house when he dropped Luke off. He knew she was probably hiding in the kitchen and just waiting for him to leave but she lied about everything now. She even got her mother to lie for her.

Maybe she was lying now when she told him she was never coming home. It was possible. You never knew with women.

That was another thing his father always said: 'You just never know what they really want, son. They probably don't even know themselves.'

Alex felt his heart lift a little.

She was lying. She really did want to come home. Her whole hissy fit was just part of some game she was playing with him.

In the quiet of the car he allowed himself a small smile. He would call her again and give her another chance. You could never take too many chances on love. He was sure that she was just waiting for him to call so she could tell him that she had lied about not coming home. That's what all those calls were about. She wanted him to know that she was ready to be with him again. She was missing Luke and she was missing him.

He had been stupid to turn off the phone but now he would make it right again.

She picked it up on the first ring.

'Hey,' he said.

'Hey,' said Liz. 'Are you okay? Is Luke okay?' Her voice was soft, pleasing. Her voice was desperate.

His heart raced with the knowledge that this was the way it

should be. He could feel the ache in his heart lift. He could feel her love over the phone.

'Yeah, he's fine. He's just having a little rest now. It's been a big day.'

He looked over at the boy. He had let him climb over into the front seat when he stopped the car and one minute they had been talking and the next Luke was asleep. He slept like he was dead. Nothing disturbed him. He was deep in his dreams and Alex loved him so much he wanted to wake him and just hold him but he had to talk to Liz now.

He knew how happy Luke would be when he told him that they were coming home again and he could go back to his old room and his old bed.

'You must be tired. He can be quite a handful.'

'I am, I guess,' he said.

'So,' she said, 'do you think you might be ready to come home now? We could get pizza and maybe watch a movie or something.' Softly pleasing. Pleasingly soft.

Alex thought about this for a moment. When they had all been together it had been his favourite time. As long as he got to pick the movie. Sometimes Liz ruined the whole thing by insisting on some feminist crap and then he had to put his foot down. Once she'd had to explain to the video guy how the disc got broken in half, but he had warned her not to choose something he wouldn't like.

He loved movie nights. They would put Luke to bed and then curl up on the sofa and feel like they were dating again. Alex would look around his house and think, 'Everything I need is right here, right now.'

'Yeah,' he said. 'That would be nice. It would be good to be together again, Liz. I think you can see now that we have to be together. If you want Luke . . . to be happy, we need to be together. If you want Luke to grow up and be a happy kid you need to put our relationship first. Do you understand what I'm saying, Liz?'

'Yes,' said Liz. 'I understand you perfectly.'

She sounded so different to the way she had sounded the last time he had called. It had been a good idea to turn the phone off.

He couldn't believe he had finally got through to her. All these months he had been trying to find the words that would make her understand that she just needed to come home and for them to be a family again and now, finally, she understood. Alex felt like he could breathe properly again. The ache on his chest lifted completely. He took a deep breath and smiled.

Keeping Luke had been the right thing to do. Liz had missed them both and now she knew it was time to come home.

'I'm glad,' he said. 'Now we can be together again. I need you to tell me that we can be together again—together forever, I mean. No more of this running away and leaving me shit.'

She was silent on the other end of the phone. She was thinking, but that was okay. He could give her time to think and time to put the words in the right order. He felt warmed by the knowledge that she was finally going to use the words, 'I'm coming home.'

He would be a better husband. He would buy flowers and try to be more patient and maybe they could have another kid so Luke had someone to play with. He was almost lost in the idea of a beach holiday for the three of them, or even just for the two of them, when Liz's voice broke in.

'Alex, I think we can talk . . .'

'Liz, I'm through with the endless discussions. You know that, don't you? I'm done talking. It's time for you to make up your mind.'

Liz was silent. Alex waited for her to say the words he needed to hear. He was patient. He could wait.

'Okay, Alex. Bring Luke back and then we can pack up our things and come home.'

'Do you mean that?' said Alex.

'Yes . . . yes I mean it.'

'Do you promise, Liz? You have to promise because otherwise I can't come back. I can't just bring Luke back and then spend another night in that empty house. Do you promise, Liz? Do you really promise?'

'Yes, Alex, I promise. Bring Luke home and everything can go back to being the way it was.'

'And I don't have to go into therapy? Promise that I won't

have to talk to some shrink, Liz, because you and I both know that there's nothing wrong with me.'

'No, Alex, you don't have to go into therapy. Just bring Luke back and it will all be all right.'

Alex felt like he could fly. After all these terrible months he had finally done it.

'Oh, Liz, I'm so . . . so . . . you just don't know how happy you've made me. We'll be a family again. A real family.'

'Yes, Alex,' said Liz. 'We'll be a family again.'

Liz didn't sound overjoyed. Her voice sounded flat. She wasn't feeling the same euphoria he was. She could have been reading her words off a card. She could have been . . .

Alex felt his body grow cold.

'Is someone there with you, Liz?'

Liz hesitated. It was just a momentary pause but Alex heard it. Then she said, 'There's no one here, Alex. It's just me and Mum. We're just waiting for you to come home with Luke.' Her voice wobbled a little. It sounded like she was trying not to cry. What was she crying about? She should have been laughing. She should have been shouting her delight to the heavens.

Maybe she didn't mean what she was saying. She could be lying again. She could be lying just to get him to bring Luke back.

'I'm going to ask you one more time, Liz, and I want you to tell me the truth. Who is there with you? Is someone telling you to say these things to me?'

'There is no one here, Alex, I promise . . . Please, just come home now. It's very late. You're very late.'

Liz was crying properly now. Alex was confused. What the fuck was she crying about?

He wanted to tell her to shut up. He wanted to yell at her to stop being so dramatic but he held the words inside. Something else was going on. He could feel it.

Who would tell her to just agree with everything he said? Who would tell her to lie and say that she was going to come home with him?

She sounded like she was being coached. She sounded like she was on television on one of those stupid cop shows. She sounded like . . .

'You're lying,' said Alex and as he said it he knew it was true.

'No, Alex—why would I lie to you? There's no one here but me and Mum. Please just come home, okay?'

In the background there was another sound that Alex couldn't quite place. It sounded like a cough. It was deep and a little rough. A man's cough. Why would Liz have a man in the house? If her father was there she could just have said. There was no way Alex wanted to run into Jack. Every time the man saw him Alex would watch him push back his shoulders and curl his fists. He didn't want to see Jack but there would be no reason for Liz to lie about him being there.

Liz was quiet on the phone. Her breathing was loud and puffed like she was running and Alex realised that she was scared. She was being so strange, so careful. Who was watching her? Who could be listening to her? And then he knew who else was there and he knew what she had done and the rage rose inside him and he wanted to pound her into the ground.

'You've called the cops,' he said. 'You've actually called the cops just because I was a little late. You stupid, stupid bitch. Who the fuck do you think you are? I have every right to keep my son for as long as I want. You can't stop me, Liz.'

'No, Alex, please. I haven't called anyone. I promise.' She was really crying hard now and then someone else took the phone and he could hear Liz's crying move into the background.

'Mr Harrow, this is Senior Constable Robert Williams from West Wood police station. You know we're here now, Mr Harrow. Please bring the boy back. Your wife is very upset. I'm sure that this will all work itself out if you come home now.'

'You can't,' said Alex, trying to stop himself from screaming at the man. 'You can't tell me to bring my son home. You have no control over me. I know my rights. A father has a right to see his son. That's the law. You can't do anything to me and you cannot tell me when I have to bring my kid home. He's my son. I bring him back when it fucking suits me.'

'Look, Mr Harrow—Alex. I know you're angry. I get that. I'm divorced too, mate, and I know how hard it can be. Why don't you just come home and we can all have a chat. It's getting close to the end of my shift. Maybe we could have a beer or something.'

Alex listened to the words and he thought that it might be nice to talk to someone who understood. None of his friends were even married. They couldn't understand why he was so hung up on Liz. He took a deep breath and then he realised that the cop was lying as well. He wasn't stupid. The man wanted him to bring Luke home and then he would help Liz make sure that Alex never saw his son again. He felt white hot fury flood his body. 'I want to talk to Liz,' he said quietly.

'Now listen, mate,' said the cop.

'I want to talk to her now,' he said.

He heard the man call for Liz and then he heard her breathe down the phone. She had stopped crying but her nose was all blocked.

'Come home, Alex,' she said.

He spoke slowly and carefully so she would know the truth. He spoke quietly so she would have to strain to hear him, and he told her. He used the words he had wanted to use since the day he came home to an empty house. Since the day he knew that another woman who was supposed to love him had left him.

'You've fucked up big time, Liz. You're going to be sorry you called the police. You're going to be sorry you left me. You're going to be sorry you took my son. For the rest of your life, every time you think of me you're going to be sorry.'

'Please, Alex . . . please, I'm begging you. Just bring him back. Nothing else matters. Please just bring him back.'

He hung up the phone then. He couldn't believe she had done that. She had no interest in getting their marriage back on track. She was probably sitting in her house with the police just laughing at how stupid he was to want her back. Well, she would be sorry. He knew that now. If he thought about it properly he had always known it. Since the day she left him and took his son he had known that one day she would be sorry for all the pain she had caused him. He knew what he needed to do. He had known all along.

He was prepared. Everything he needed was already in the car—had been for months now. Some days he needed to know it was there just so he could make it through to the other end.

It was her fault. If she had loved him the way she was supposed to, if she had been a better woman and a better wife, she would have been able to live a happy life with him—but that was all over now. She had betrayed him.

The betrayal sat heavily on him. He wanted to cry but he had no tears left for Liz. He had no tears left for himself. He was overcome by a weariness that he knew he would never be able to shake. She was never coming back to him and she was never coming home. The years laid themselves out before him, threaded through with petty arguments about pick-up times and who paid for what. The loneliness was a taste in his mouth. He couldn't do this anymore. He couldn't go on.

It was quiet in the park. The cold had driven everyone inside and his was the only car around. He was probably not allowed to park here under the trees but fuck them. Fuck them all. He had driven over the oval and into the small canopy of trees at the back. Without knowing why, he had felt the need to hide. He enjoyed the feel of the grass under his wheels. The runners would be pissed at the mess in the morning. They would stand in their stupid shorts and shake their heads at the tragedy of their messed-up oval, not realising that just under the trees there was a man with a broken heart and a broken soul.

He turned on his phone again and dialled his father.

His father hadn't liked Liz much.

'She reminds me of your mother. They both have that way of looking down on you, like you're a piece of shit.'

'Liz is not like that, Dad,' Alex had said.

'You think that now, boy, but just you wait. She's pretty full of her own opinions. Women like that are hard work.'

Alex had laughed at his father then. Laughed at him, sure in the knowledge of the love he and Liz had for each other. He had known then that there was nothing they could not face together, no problem they couldn't get through. What did he know now?

'Nothing,' he whispered into the fusty air of the car. 'Nothing at all.'

12

'Hey, boy,' said his father when he answered the phone.

'Hey, Dad. How have you been?'

'You know. Can't complain. What's up?'

Alex tried to imagine his father as he would be now. He would be sitting in his favourite chair with a beer or he would be fixing something in the house. His father had gone crazy fixing things after his mother left. Doors that jammed and windows that stuck were sanded and moved until they were perfect. Light bulbs blew and were replaced immediately. Catches and hooks were screwed in correctly and a new fence appeared in the garden. He fixed at night, sometimes waking Alex. Sometimes Alex was the helper and the two of them had made the house perfect. Everywhere

Alex looked there was order and perfection. His father seemed soothed by the act of restoring the house.

Alex could not remember his father ever having done anything in the house before his mother left. He remembered his mother making lists and putting them up on the fridge but his father just took them down and threw them away. 'I work hard enough,' he would say. 'I'll get to this stuff when I'm good and ready.'

After she had left he had made his own lists and crossed off each chore with a thick black marker, obliterating the words underneath.

Alex had supposed at the time that he was lucky. There were worse things his father could have done than fix the house and have a bad day every now and again.

His father never drank so much that he couldn't function and there was always a meal on the table at dinner time. But there were the bad days. Days when his father could find nothing to fix or clean were bad days. Those were the days Alex retreated to his room, where even the books on the bookcase were perfectly aligned.

Alex could picture his father now with hair that used to look like his but was now grey and thin. His father might know what he could do about the ache on his chest and Liz who was so cold she'd called the police on him.

'I just wanted to talk to you, Dad . . . I just . . . I don't know.'

'Alex, I'm in the middle of something here. Maybe you could come round for a beer later?'

'No, Dad . . . I don't think that later would be good. I don't feel so good, Dad.'

'What do you mean? Are you sick?'

Alex laughed. 'Sometimes I think I *am* sick, Dad. Not the kind of sick you mean. I'm just so . . . so . . . sad and I don't know how to stop feeling this way. It's hard to breathe and there's an ache across my chest. I feel like I can't take this anymore. I can't be away from her and Luke. I just can't. I don't know how to . . . to . . . be.'

'Come on, boy, that's ridiculous. You need to pull yourself up by your bootstraps and get on with things. I told you that woman was no good for you. It's the best thing that could have happened. You can move on with your life now. Find someone who really appreciates you. Find a woman who can make you happy. Let go of that Liz, Alex. She wasn't right for you from the start. You have to be strong, Alex. You have to be in control. You have to set a good example for that boy of yours. Weren't you supposed to see him today?'

'I was . . . I mean I am. He's here with me now. He was supposed to be home hours ago but I just wanted to keep him with me. I should have taken him home but I don't want to and Liz keeps calling and now she's called the cops on me.'

'Called the cops? What the fuck for?'

'She wants me to bring Luke home. She's angry that I'm late.'

'So you're a little late—the cops must have laughed at her. Don't worry about that, boy. They can't touch you just because your wife is crazy. She really needs to be put in her place, that one.'

'How did you do it, Dad?'

'How did I do what?'

'How did you survive after Mum left? How did you go on? I can't see how I can go on, Dad. I loved her so much and she's left me and I know that she's going to turn Luke against me. I can already feel it happening. In a few years he won't want to talk to me. I'm going to be left with nothing again, Dad, and I don't think I can stand it.'

'Steady on now, Alex. This kind of talk is just rubbish. Liz can't take him away from you. There's such a thing as a father's rights, you know.'

'How did you do it, Dad?'

'I don't . . . oh Jesus, Alex, I don't know. We weren't getting along too good before she left. I guess I thought it was a bit of a blessing really. We muddled along okay, didn't we? We did all right?'

Alex didn't know how to answer the question. Muddling along wasn't the same as being all right. They hadn't been all right. Frank had gone to work and Alex had gone to school and they had tidied and cleaned and fixed and, as Frank put it, 'muddled along', but they were just pretending. Alex had never been allowed to shed a tear for what he had lost, had never been allowed to talk about her, and even as a kid he had felt his heart weigh him down. His mother's absent presence filled every room. Each time his father changed something in the house or threw out something that had belonged to her she took up more space in the house.

'Yeah . . . I guess, but I was a sad kid, Dad. I know you were trying to do your best but I felt like there was something sitting on my chest for years. We should have talked about her. She should have visited me or written letters or something. Why didn't she want to see me?'

'Alex, you're a grown man and you sound like a whining child. You need to leave the past where it is, son.'

'You know she has a whole new family. I found her picture on Facebook. She's got other kids and everything.'

Frank was quiet for a moment. 'Did you contact her?' he asked.

Alex sighed. He knew what his father was asking. He wasn't asking about him and his mother. He wanted to know if Alex had spoken to his mother and if she had said anything about him. Frank wanted his secrets to stay buried, along with the memory of his wife.

'I didn't contact her, Dad. What would be the point? If she had wanted to be a mother to me she would have made sure that we stayed in contact.'

'Quite right,' said Frank. 'She was a selfish woman and I know you may not believe me, but she wasn't a very good mother either.'

'Good mothers don't leave their children.'

'Exactly. Now, boy, you need to let all this go. You need to find yourself a pretty girl and, you know, bonk her brains out. You need to go out and laugh and drink and just leave Liz to do what she wants with her life.'

'But Liz made me feel better. She was the one who saved me. I know you don't like her but she lifted the stone off my chest and made me feel alive. She made me so happy, Dad. We were supposed to be the perfect family. And now she's a complete bitch. She's so cold and so harsh and she hates me so much. I can't take it, Dad.'

'Look, Alex, why don't you come over for a beer? I know she's a bitch. I always said that. Give me a few minutes to finish up what I'm doing and then we'll have a beer. You can bring your little lad and Liz can just wait until you're good and ready to bring him back.'

Alex thought about the taste of a cold beer on his tongue but he had no desire for it. He had no desire for anything. He could see his future as one long dark tunnel. He couldn't see any light; he couldn't even see the possibility of a light.

'I bought a gun, Dad.'

'Jesus, Alex, what the fuck for?'

Alex knew he didn't have to answer the question. His father knew what the gun was for.

'For protection,' he said.

'Where would you get a gun, Alex? Guns are illegal.'

'Yeah, well, I know someone who knows someone. You know how it goes.'

'If the cops know you have a gun you'll be up for it, Alex. You know that, don't you?'

'I do, Dad, but . . . I don't think I care anymore. I just don't give a fuck anymore.'

'Now look here, Alex—you don't want to be doing anything stupid. Come over here and we'll talk. We'll figure this out. Barbara will make us all a nice meal.'

'I don't think so, Dad. I just want to be with my boy. I wish I'd never met her, Dad. Then I wouldn't have to feel this pain.'

'Alex, where is this gun?'

'It's here with me, Dad. In the car.'

'Alex, just come over here now. Please, you have to listen to me—just come now. Or I can come to you. Tell me where you are and I'll come get you both. We can go down to the pub and order a pizza. We can give your little lad his first sip of beer. That will really piss off that wife of yours. Come on, Alex, don't be a fool, boy. Tell me where you are and I'll come get you.'

'I don't think so, Dad. I'll see you, okay? I love you, Dad. I know you did your best.'

'Alex, just listen . . .'

'Bye, Dad.'

Alex switched off the phone again. His father couldn't help him. No one could help him. Luke's breathing was slow and even. He had to make the pain stop but he couldn't think how to do it. He just couldn't organise his thoughts into a straight line.

13

Frank frantically dialled Alex. He dialled once, twice, three times and then he gave up. 'What the fuck is going on?' he thought. What on earth was Alex talking about?

He was probably just having a bad day. Frank remembered the bad days after Margaret left. They came at you out of the blue. One morning he would just wake up and feel this terrible sadness take hold of his body.

'Maybe I should call that Liz,' he thought and then he shook his head. He had never had a real conversation with his former daughter-in-law. What on earth could he say to her now? He really didn't fucking need this crap now. He was trying to fix the handle on the door Barbara kept going on about and he wanted to get it done before the match started. She had stood with her hands on her hips that morning and said, 'That door handle better bloody be fixed by the time I get back, Frank.'

The handle had been sticking and difficult to move for two months and when Barbara's hands went on her hips Frank knew she meant business. The thing about the handle was that it wasn't really broken. All you had to do was jiggle it a certain way and it worked perfectly. It wasn't his fault that Barbara had no idea how to move the thing.

Frank had just given her a look and she had shut her mouth and left but he thought he might as well do the handle. A man could go crazy being nagged about the same things all day every day.

He didn't understand Alex. Why couldn't the boy just let go of that woman? He had always been a bit of a clinger, especially when it came to women. Even when he was ten and had a little girlfriend, he didn't seem to be able to give her enough space. The mother eventually called Frank and asked him to put a stop to the phone calls and the way Alex followed the girl around the playground. Frank had laughed at the woman but he had told Alex to back off.

Alex had been devastated. Frank remembered him spending whole weekends in his room and only wanting to eat cake. The boy had a strange love of cake. Some weeks he couldn't get enough and then there would be times when he went for months without it. He hadn't wanted any since he met Liz. He wouldn't even eat a piece of the wedding cake. Everyone had laughed about him wanting to look good for his bride but Frank could see people found it a bit strange.

People had always found Alex a bit strange. He lied a lot when he was a kid and he couldn't understand why the lies pissed people off. It was like he just didn't get it. A good belting had always sorted him out for a few months but it was like the kid was addicted to creating stories about his life. The teachers at school had told Frank more than once that they thought therapy would be a good idea but there was no way he would do that to Alex. People went into therapy with some small problem and landed up spending their whole lives whining about everything. Frank didn't want that for Alex. Alex needed to be strong. Neither of them had needed to blub to some stranger about how they felt after Margaret left. They had needed to find a way forward. They had managed, hadn't they?

Alex would be fine if he just got out of his empty house and found himself a new life.

He needed to get on with things and leave Liz behind.

It was never good for a man to get so attached to a woman. Frank knew that even before Margaret had upped and left for who knew where.

He had managed to let go of Margaret all right. The day after she left he had cleared the house of everything that reminded him of her. She'd left a whole lot of clothes and knick knacks and bits of crap and he'd just gone through the house and tossed out every single piece. Occasionally he would find something that he'd missed and out it would go. He enjoyed watching the things she'd loved crack and crumble when he tossed them in the garbage. They did without teacups for a few months rather than save the ones she had inherited from her mother. It wasn't like they were giving many tea parties anyway.

If she ever came crawling back he would show her that she'd been wiped from their lives without a second thought. He wanted her to know that she meant nothing to him. He wanted her to know that he and Alex were getting on with their lives as though she had never even existed.

During the day he managed to pretend he was okay with it all. At work the ex-wife jokes rolled off his tongue. 'Me and the boy are doing just fine,' he told anyone who would listen. He kept the house well oiled and running smoothly. Alex never went to school dirty and the boy knew how to clean up after himself by the time he was seven. At night things were a little different. Then he would have to look at Alex, who had her eyes. At night, sometimes he forgot to hold on to his disdain and some memories would creep in and screw him up. Alex had her way of looking at him, like she was confused about something. It drove him a bit crazy.

He could feel the boy's desperation and longing for his mother but he couldn't give in to it. He wanted him to grow up to be stronger than his father was. She should have taken Alex. What kind of a mother just abandons her son?

Someone who wasn't capable of loving anyone but her own selfish self, that was for sure. He hadn't meant it when he said he would track her down and kill her if she took the boy. It was all just talk, really. That's what men did. It didn't have to mean anything.

Margaret was just another cunt looking to control some man, like Liz. Jesus, women were difficult. Barbara said that he could do as he pleased and that all she wanted to do was take care of him, but here he was trying to fix a door handle that didn't really need fixing in time for the match. He looked at his watch. He'd missed the first few minutes already.

All a man really wanted was a bit of peace, but women couldn't let go. If he could have lived without sex he would have done just fine. Your cock got you into all sorts of trouble. God that Liz was a bitch. Imagine calling the cops just because Alex was a bit late bringing the boy back. He could understand why Alex felt the need to give her a bit of a smack now and then. He'd said as much to Barbara when Alex told them what Liz was saying about him and Barbara had gone all funny. 'So you think it's okay to hit a woman, do you, Frank?' she'd said, and then she'd gone to bed and refused to talk to him.

'I didn't say it was okay,' he told her the next morning. 'I just said that with someone like that Liz I could understand it.'

A man could only be pushed so far and that was the truth. He never told Barbara that there had been times when Margaret had pushed him a little too much. He didn't like to think about it now but there had been the odd smack or two. He just got a little angry with her and it had only happened a few times. Of course he'd said he was sorry afterwards and he really had been. He never wanted to hurt Margaret or Alex, but wives and kids were the same really. They needed to learn.

He'd never raise his hand to Barbara, of course. She'd probably kill him in his sleep if he tried any funny business with her. He quite liked that about her. Margaret had moaned a lot and cried a lot. It was enough to drive a bloke mad.

What was it with women? If you went out and did a fair day's work you were entitled to be left alone when you needed a bit of time to relax. Women just didn't get it.

Frank put down the screwdriver. The handle was old and the screw was stripped. Bloody thing wouldn't come out. He should have told Alex to come over and help him. Not that he needed help with something so small but maybe if the boy had something to do with his hands he wouldn't be thinking all these things. It was all very well to get yourself an education but Frank believed that if your hands were busy your mind could just rest. That's what he'd done after Margaret left. He'd fixed everything in the house—even remodelled the bathroom. All the shit she used to nag him about got done. He wanted to call her up and say, 'See? All you had to do was stop nagging.'

Margaret would probably just have laughed at him. He pitied the poor bloke she'd managed to catch after she left.

She had sent stuff to Alex over the years but Frank knew that the boy needed to move on. He'd tossed it all in the bin without a second thought. There was no way he was going to make it easy for her to have a relationship with Alex. If she wanted to see the boy she could bloody well come back from wherever it was and see him. After about five years nothing came through the mail anymore.

He had done his best. Alex thought he'd been a sad kid but he was wrong. They'd both been fine. They'd done all right. There were difficult days but everyone had those—and what kid hadn't had a few smacks over time? Alex did him proud in the end. After he got kicked out of that one school for fighting they'd had a long talk about the future and Frank had set him on the straight and narrow.

He straightened up again and stretched his back. Alex wasn't serious about the gun, was he? He wouldn't do anything to himself or . . . or Luke?

Frank rubbed his eyes and took a deep breath. In the first days after Margaret had left he had wished Alex had gone with her. Kids were too much fucking work. He had wished the boy gone a few times over the years but it wasn't like he'd ever done anything about it.

He should probably give Liz a call. She didn't deserve a phone call, of course. She had never been known to give him the time of day.

Still, Alex did say he had a gun, and maybe that was all just talk but it was pretty easy to get a gun these days. In the pub a few weeks ago he'd gone to have a piss and walked in on two guys exchanging a package that looked a bit big to have drugs in it. He'd pretended to be drunker than he was and the blokes had written him off as harmless and left. It was only a suburban pub and there was all sorts of shit going on when the night headed towards dawn.

If she had called the cops already they could help find Alex and then maybe they could have a beer together and talk this thing through.

He could just keep quiet about it and let Alex sort it out, but the boy sounded a bit down—well, more than a bit really. He wouldn't do anything stupid, though, would he? Nah, Alex would take the kid back soon and then the cops couldn't do anything. Frank would call him later and they would have a talk. In the meantime, he should just leave well enough alone.

He really needed to get this door handle done. He tried another screwdriver but it still wouldn't work. The screw extractor was at work. The repair would have to wait whether or not Barbara liked it.

He needed a smoke but he didn't feel like going outside. Barbara had recently decided that they should only smoke outside. The house stank and Luke didn't like coming over because of it. Barbara had really taken to Luke like he was her own grandson. He was a brilliant little kid and it was so much easier to relax when you weren't responsible for the big stuff. Luke liked to follow him with his plastic tool set when he fixed things and he talked all the time. He didn't mind if you answered him or not. He just liked to talk.

The kid had been so excited when Frank had given him the plastic tool set. His eyes had lit up like he'd been given the moon. The boy had such a great smile. Alex told him the kid slept with the plastic tool set for three days. Luke looked just like Alex too. It made Frank remember the good times, before Margaret had left.

What if Alex was really in a bad way? If something happened the cops would know that Alex had called him. Big Brother was everywhere these days. He wouldn't want to be the person who could have done something and didn't. No one wants to be that person. Maybe it would be better to tell someone what Alex had said. He probably didn't even have a gun.

Frank sighed. All he had really wanted to do was watch the match and have a quiet beer.

He would call Liz and mention the gun, just in case. He didn't want anything to happen to the boy.

If Alex got angry later he would say that he had just been taking precautions. 'I know you wouldn't do anything stupid,' he would tell Alex. 'But you sounded . . . you know, upset and I was just playing it safe.' Alex would understand.

He went downstairs to the living room where Liz's mother's number was in the book. He was just taking precautions, just playing it safe. It was good to play it safe. He would just mention the gun. Alex would understand. He would keep the conversation short. It was her fault, really—all of it. She was the one who had upset Alex. She was the reason he bought a gun. Jesus, he really hoped the boy wouldn't do anything stupid. He cleared his throat, ready to speak. He would just mention the gun and then he could relax.

The phone barely got to finish its first ring. Her mother answered and he didn't make small talk. He just asked to speak to Liz.

'Hello, Liz, this is Frank. I think there's something you should know.'

Two hours late

Robert put his cup in the sink. Liz was sitting in the armchair again and her eyes were closed. He couldn't imagine what she was thinking. They had well and truly messed up. He didn't know how the father had heard Dave cough. They hadn't really been taking this seriously enough. They hadn't been treating this like a hostage negotiation and maybe it was.

But just maybe it wasn't. The father had sounded upset and more than a little whacko but he could just be mouthing off. There could be other stuff going on. The press would love that. He could almost see the headline now: POLICE WASTE TIME AT DOMESTIC WHILE SHOPKEEPER MURDERED, or something like that.

Robert had been relieved when the phone rang, hoping that the father would say he was bringing the kid home, but when Liz had hesitated he'd mouthed that she should agree to whatever he wanted. Then it had all gone wrong anyway.

Liz looked worn down by years of confrontations with the man. Sometimes marriage was just tiring. You came home to the same person and the same argument dressed up as money or the kids or the holiday you needed to have but it was all basically the same. Sometimes you came home to a fist and Robert could see how Liz would want to avoid that now that she had managed to leave the arsehole.

But leaving the arsehole didn't always mean leaving the confrontation and the fist. The pile of AVOs the court had to get through every day could attest to that.

Robert speaking to the man might have done some good in this situation. There was a chance that Alex would have got a bit of a fright knowing the police were involved. Most of these men were only filled with bravado until another man stepped in. Out in the world they were cowards who truly believed they got pushed around. They went home to find someone they could stamp all over and make themselves feel like men again. It was pathetic really, but the ego was bound up in everything.

Of course, if Alex was in a dark place then nothing anyone said could change what he was thinking or planning.

After the call, Robert had let the station know that the bloke had threatened his wife.

Lisa told him she would radio the rego number to everyone on duty. Not that 'you'll be sorry' actually constituted a threat. Natalie had told him he'd be sorry every day for at least a year before they separated.

Legally the guy had still done nothing wrong. If he walked in right now they could caution him or drag him down to the station and throw him in a cell for an hour or so, but being late and being a complete dickhead to your wife were not crimes, else they'd all be in jail.

If Liz hadn't bothered to call the police an hour ago and only just called now she would have probably had to wait awhile for someone to come out. Shift change was coming up and the situation was only urgent to Liz.

But here they were, and now that he had heard the guy on the phone, now that he could see how anxious Liz was, he was glad they had come. At least now Liz felt like they had tried to help.

The press loved to make the police out to be a bunch of slackers. Every time something happened and they weren't on the scene within five minutes there would be articles about how long it took them to get there or how long it took them to put out an alert or how long it took them to catch the guy. The public wanted you there before it happened, and now here they were and Robert could sense the situation unfolding. He didn't know which way things were going to go yet but he had a feeling, just a twist of the gut really, that told him it wasn't going to end well.

So now everyone was looking and maybe they should have been looking before but he didn't want to get the rest of the force involved without a good reason.

He had radioed in the guy's mobile phone number and Lisa was trying to get a fix on the nearest tower. That would give them a better idea of where the guy was now. He had switched off the phone again but they'd get close enough.

Dave came into the kitchen.

'What are we going to do, Rob? Our shift is over soon. Do we stay? Do we tell the night guys to come and relieve us?'

'Fuck, Dave, I just don't know. This feels like something— doesn't it feel like something?'

'Maybe,' said Dave. 'But the chances are we're just in the middle of some argument the dickhead and his wife have been having for the last five years.'

'She says he's always on time. She keeps stressing that. I don't think he's ever been late before.'

'Being late is not a crime,' said Dave.

'I know that, Dave, but we need to think this through. The guy is never late and from what she says he's all about control. Why would he be doing this now?'

'He's just trying to piss her off.'

'No,' said Robert. 'I think it's more than that. He sounded really weird on the phone. He sounded like he was losing it.'

'Yeah, well, we still need to go back to the station and put together some kind of report.'

'Yeah, probably best if we check in. You can go on home after that. I'll come back here and see how this pans out.'

'I'm not going to let you go it alone, Rob. If you come back I'll come back.'

'I've trained you well.'

'You've trained me to appreciate a cold beer.'

Robert laughed. 'Okay, let's go and tell them.'

In the living room the friend called Rhonda was explaining to someone on the phone that she wouldn't be home.

'I'm not asking you to keep them for longer, Dan, I'm just telling you to drop them at Mum's place. Yeah it is important and no I'm not going to explain it. Do me a favour and try to be less of a wanker—and before you tell me that you're going to smack me head in why don't I pass you over to the nice policeman next to me and you can explain it to him? Thanks, Dan, I thought you'd be happy to drop them at Mum's.'

She ended the call and raised her eyebrows at Robert, who put up his hands.

'One problem at a time,' he said to her.

'I'm not asking for your help,' said Rhonda. 'I figured out a long time ago that I was basically on my own.'

Robert sighed and shook his head. He turned to the woman in the armchair.

'Look, Liz, we'll go back to the station now and see if we can get any more information on the car. We have people looking and we're trying to use the mobile phone towers to get a fix on his location. He still hasn't done anything we can charge him with, but we will try to get him to come home when we find him. I'm sorry, but at the moment it's the best we can do.'

'That's okay,' said Liz. Her voice was low and drained of emotion.

He could see that she didn't want them to leave.

'Everyone on duty is out looking, Mrs Harrow,' said Dave. 'They'll find them. He can't have gone that far and the chances are that when your son needs dinner and needs to get to bed, he'll bring him home.'

'You have both our numbers,' said Robert. 'We'll be back in about an hour. If he calls you or returns the boy, please let us know right away.'

She nodded and Robert could see that she was hanging on to every word they were saying.

She was holding her mobile phone and when the home phone rang she nearly hit the roof.

It wasn't her ex-husband. Her mother gave her the phone and she greeted the caller formally, politely and without any warmth. Her mother stood next to her trying to hear what was being said.

Robert and Dave lifted their hands to say goodbye and went

to the front door. Robert felt bad about leaving now but they weren't getting anything done sitting here.

Alex Harrow sounded like an educated man. If he knew the cops had been called he probably knew it would be a good idea to get the kid home.

The sun was setting and the autumn cold was getting everyone ready for winter. Robert could almost taste a cold beer in a warm pub but he would have to put that off for later. He wondered how long this would go on. He wasn't up for spending the night in the house trying to get everyone to calm down.

'I was supposed to have a date tonight,' said Dave as they closed the front door behind them.

'Yeah, well, if she's going to date a cop the sooner she gets used to dates being cancelled the better.'

'Jeez, jaded much,' said Dave.

Robert gave him a grim smile. Dave was so young.

They were halfway down the front path when the door opened and Liz came running out. She was still holding the cordless phone. 'Wait,' she called, her voice high and anxious.

Her face was milky white against the orange afternoon and her lips were trembling. She was holding the cordless phone out to them, offering them her explanation.

Dave ended his call to his pissed off date and walked towards her, catching her as she stumbled.

'What's wrong?' Robert asked.

'The phone . . . it was Alex's father. Frank. Alex called him.' She was speaking quickly, stumbling over the words. 'Alex called him a few minutes ago. He called to tell him . . . to tell him . . . Oh Jesus, oh Jesus, my little boy.'

'Mrs Harrow, please,' said Dave. 'Tell us what he said.'

'Alex has a gun,' she said. 'He has a gun.'

'Fuck,' whispered Dave. He stepped forward as Liz's legs buckled beneath her, and helped her up the path towards the house.

'Fuck,' thought Robert. 'Game changer.'

He radioed the station. 'Hey, Lisa,' he said. 'We need to get some choppers in the air. Things just got serious. I'll call you back in a few minutes. Get them up there now, Lisa—the guy's got a gun.'

Inside the house Robert and Dave could hear Liz's mother shouting and her two friends talking in soothing voices.

'Fuck,' thought Robert. 'Fuck, fuck, fuck.'

Liz was still holding the phone and Robert could hear a man's voice on the other end.

'Hello, Liz? Liz, are you there?'

'This is Senior Constable Robert Williams—can you tell me who I'm speaking with, please?'

'Ah . . . well . . . it's Frank, Frank Harrow. Alex is my son.'

'Mr Harrow, how do you know that your son is in possession of a gun?'

'He . . . ah . . . he told me and I just thought you . . . well I thought Liz should know.'

'When did he tell you, Mr Harrow?'

'Now . . . just now. Well, about twenty minutes ago. He called me and we were talking and he told me about the gun.'

'Did he mention his son? Did he mention Luke?'

'Yes . . . yes he did. Luke is with him. They're in the car but he didn't say where. He told me he has a gun in the car and I got worried for him and for . . . for Luke.'

'Mr Harrow, did he sound upset to you? Did he make any threats?'

'He didn't make any threats but yes . . . yes he is upset. It's that wife of his, you see. I told him he would be better off without her but he didn't seem to want to listen.'

'Mr Harrow, did he threaten to harm Luke or himself?'

The man on the other end of the phone gave a long sigh. Robert could sense that he was buying time, trying to figure out the correct answer.

'Mr Harrow, you have to tell me the truth. Your grandson may be in danger and your son may be a danger to himself. You have to tell me the truth.'

'I don't know,' said Frank Harrow and Robert heard him swallow quickly. 'I just . . . he seemed so upset. He seemed really sad and he said he doesn't know how to live without Liz. He's not good. He told me he wasn't good.'

'Mr Harrow, do you have any idea where he might be? Any idea at all? Is there a place he likes to take Luke to that Liz doesn't know about?'

'No . . . I'm sorry, I don't know. I know they like the park but it's too cold now to be outside. Alex wouldn't have Luke outside. He's a good dad. Alex is a really good dad and he loves Luke. He wouldn't do anything to hurt him. I know that he loves him too much to hurt him. He's just feeling a bit sad at the moment because of the divorce and all. He's a good boy is Alex. He's never been in trouble before except for the usual boy stuff and now he's just a bit sad. He'll bring Luke home soon. I tried to get him to come here but he didn't want to. I said we could have a beer.'

'Mr Harrow, could you give me your address, please? I'm going to send over some other constables so they can be with you if your son calls again.'

Robert wrote down the address and handed it to Dave, who was already on the phone talking to the station. At least they were here. At least people were already looking. At least there was a chance they'd find this kid before his father did something to him or to both of them. Why the fuck did this keep happening? If you put together the gun and the things the man had said to his wife you had real threats and real problems. Just having a gun meant the bloke was up shit creek. At least if he came home now they would be able to hold him for longer.

Maybe the man wasn't just blowing hot air. Robert rubbed his face and wished the cold beer goodbye. He would need to call the higher-ups and it might not be a bad idea to let the media unit know. They could put the word out. Might as well have the whole state looking for this dickhead.

Liz had resumed her position in the armchair. For such a tall woman she seemed to have shrunk into the soft leather. She wasn't crying. Robert didn't know if it was shock or something else but she wasn't crying.

'Now you're going to stay,' she said. Her voice was flat. It wasn't a question. It was just a fact and in it were all the other things she wanted to say. Now they were going to stay so they would be with her when they found her son and they would be with her when he came home or when he didn't come home. Now they would stay even though now it could be too late. Now they were going to stay.

14

'Can I get you something else to drink, Mrs Harrow?' said Dave.

Liz looked up at him. She had been thinking about cake and he startled her into shame. She should have been thinking about Luke. Instead she had been thinking about the cake she had eaten with tea this morning when she and her mother had thought they only had a few hours until their lives were once again subject to the demands of a child. She had felt guilty about the piece of cake but now she wondered briefly if she would ever eat again. Her mother had pushed the diet this morning but now seemed only interested in getting her to open her lips for food. Ellen was in the kitchen making one sandwich after another, filling platters and plates with perfect triangles.

It was the nature of a mother to feed her child. Liz had never understood it until she had Luke, but now she knew that if Luke was eating he was basically fine. When he was off his food it was time to call the doctor. Her mother needed her to be fine, even though they both knew that it was never going to be fine again. Rebecca kept throwing positive clichés out into the air but no one was listening anymore.

No one knew what to say about the gun. Guns belonged on television shows and on the news. Guns belonged in the Cross where drugs were sold. No one knew what to say about the gun.

'What a difference a day makes,' thought Liz without a trace of humour.

The police officers had covered themselves with a professional veneer after the phone call from Frank. They had begun to ask difficult questions and even to push her a little bit. Liz wanted to shout, 'Where was all this concern before?' but her throat closed over and she swallowed her words. They had only been doing the right thing. They had asked the questions, but now the gun had changed everything. A gun meant that Alex was not just a threat to himself and to Luke but to the wider public.

A week ago there had been a story on television about a man who had a gun and when the police caught up with him he had waved it in their direction and now he was dead. The police didn't fuck around when a gun was in the picture. Liz liked the idea of Alex getting shot by the police. She liked the idea of him dying in a car crash or jumping off a bridge. She just wanted him gone. Right now she didn't care that his child would grow up without a father, she just needed him to be gone and her little boy to be here eating fish sticks with too much tomato sauce or pulling olives off his pizza so he could eat those first.

As long as Luke came home safe she liked the idea of Alex's death more with each passing minute.

Her world felt tilted. If she stood up she got dizzy so she was staying put in the chair. Everything was out of kilter. Her child couldn't be locked in a car with someone who had a gun, could he? It was not her reality. It could not be her reality, she could not bear it.

She had written down all the places Alex might have taken Luke. She had called all Alex's friends and some work colleagues that were listed in her contacts on her phone. She had called a few of the mothers from Luke's old playgroup even though Luke no longer attended because he was at preschool.

'Oh, Liz,' said Melissa. 'We haven't heard from you in an age.' Liz hadn't the patience to keep talking so she threw in her question about Alex and Luke and then Melissa got all emotional and started crying. Liz wanted to reach through the phone and strangle her. The impulse left her shaking and nauseous.

The gun had changed everything. Now he was on the wrong side of the law. The man who threw his daughter off a bridge had been doing nothing wrong until the moment he stepped out of his car and hurled the small child to her death. By then it was too late of course. She supposed she should be grateful that the police had even listened to her when she first called. It must be the hardest part of the job, figuring out what to take seriously and what to dismiss.

After she had called everyone she could think of she had detailed every abusive incident for Robert so he could try to figure out a pattern of triggers for Alex's anger. He wanted to know about every bruise, every put-down and every tear she had shed.

They had sat in the dining room, away from the others, and Liz had been grateful for the small measure of privacy. She had felt stripped naked and the words had come while she twisted her hands and studied her mother's rose embroidered table cloth as she went over the events of the night before again and again, repeating every word she had said, every move she had made.

She had no idea what Robert was listening for but she kept talking.

But now there was nothing left to say. The television was on the news channel but the volume was too low for anyone to hear anything. Running at the bottom of the screen was a continuous loop of text.

If anyone has seen or sees a blue Toyota sedan licence plate WVX217 contact police immediately. Do not approach the vehicle.

If anyone has seen or sees a blue Toyota sedan licence plate WVX217 contact police immediately. Do not approach the vehicle.

If anyone has seen or sees a blue Toyota sedan licence plate WVX217 contact police immediately. Do not approach the vehicle.

The whole state was now looking for Alex and Luke. The whole state and still they'd heard nothing in the last twenty minutes. How could that be?

Robert said that the media would arrive soon so she could make a plea to Alex to come home. He could be somewhere and see a television.

'You never know,' Robert had said.

'No,' agreed Liz. 'You never do.'

Liz felt her skin crawl at the thought of having to go on television and bare her soul for people tucking into their takeaway food. She would look shocking. Her face was pale and blotchy and her hair was greasy because she couldn't stop running her hands through it. She wondered at herself for even thinking about the way she looked but vanity would not be silenced by her distress. She would stand naked on television if it meant Luke would come home safe. She would stand naked or she would let Alex shoot her. Could she say that on television? Could she say, 'Alex, if you just bring Luke home I will stand in the front yard of my mother's house and let you shoot me or I will let you beat me until you cannot lift your arms anymore. If you just bring him home safe I will let you do whatever you want.'

She tried to swallow the churning emotions because she was afraid she would burst into flames.

She thought about the cake she had eaten this morning and regretted not having cream with it.

Rhonda and Rebecca were leafing through old magazines or taking it in turns to make tea and coffee so they could all drown their sorrows.

Liz wanted them to leave—all of them. She wanted to be alone so she could find the thread and unravel how she had got herself here.

Every mistake she had made, starting with the first cup of coffee she had ever shared with Alex, lined up and marched towards her. She closed her eyes and wished them away but still they came and she knew that at every turn she could have prevented this from happening.

If she had told him 'no' she couldn't go out with him, this wouldn't have happened.

If she had left after he threw the socks at her, this wouldn't have happened.

If she had never agreed to marry him, this wouldn't have happened.

If she had left after the first time he shoved her, this wouldn't have happened.

If she had said 'no' he couldn't come over last night, this wouldn't have happened.

One night, after Alex had hit her on her side so hard Liz thought he might have broken a rib, she sat up all night in pain, trying to breathe and thinking about ways to kill him. She was sure that her father would know someone who knew someone who could do it for her, although she didn't really want to get her father involved. She had gone down to the kitchen and studied the knives, wondering which one would be strong enough to push through his ribs and into his heart. She had looked under the sink and wondered which poison would be undetectable in coffee and she had wondered if she had the courage to hold a pillow over his face if she'd hit him with something heavy first.

She had watched the sun come up without doing anything, of course, and in the morning he had been completely devastated that she had not been able to sleep. He had taken the day off and looked after Luke and cooked and cleaned and allowed her to rest. There was nothing to be done for a broken rib anyway except rest but even if there had been there was no possibility of a visit to the doctor. By the end of the week Liz was feeling better and Alex was firmly entrenched in the loving phase and she forgot about her urge to end his life.

But as she sat now and thought about cake she knew that if she had gone through with her impulse that night, if she had managed to end his life or even hurt him enough to cripple him, this would not have happened.

She curled her body up into the old leather armchair her father had left behind when he moved out. Her mother had tried to throw it out but it was the one thing Liz got hysterical about.

The chair smelled of her father. He had seeped into the leather. It was the one chair in the house in which she was completely comfortable. Her mother had tried to make Liz take it to her own house but Alex hated the chair for the very reason that Liz loved it. It was a large wingback with metal studs on the body and a soft cushion on the seat. Alex looked small in the chair. He had only ever sat in it once, making Ellen laugh. Jack filled the chair, as did Liz.

Her father had come back about ten minutes after they had heard from Frank. She had watched his fist curl when her mother told him about the gun. His face had coloured and she could see him counting in his head, trying to hold back his fury.

Her mother had taken him off to the kitchen and Liz knew she was telling him the tale of his daughter's marriage. Liz knew her mother would start at the beginning, but it was not the real beginning. Ellen only knew what Liz had allowed her to know but it was enough for her father to get the picture. Enough to devastate him.

Liz knew Ellen was letting him know that his daughter had stayed with a man who hurt her and that she had never come to him to ask for help. When he came back from the kitchen he had patted her on the head but he hadn't been able to find any words to console her.

Now he sat on the couch trying to fill in the silence that he usually loved. He sounded awkward and suddenly, in the face of what was about to happen, he looked very small. He couldn't save her from this. No one could save her from this. She had let her baby go and now she was going to lose him. The knowledge of that loss filled her body with acid. She was never going to see him again.

'Sorry . . . ?' she said, realising Dave was speaking.

'I asked if I could get you a drink, Mrs Harrow. Um, some tea or something.'

Liz smiled up at him. His face was twisted into a sad smile and he was slouching slightly like he was trying to fit his tall, skinny frame into the room. Liz felt his awkwardness as her own. 'Please call me Liz,' she said.

'Liz, can I get you anything?' said Dave.

'Thanks, yeah, that would be nice.' She didn't think she could swallow any more liquid.

Dave nodded and Liz could see that he was glad to have something to do. His partner Robert was in charge of taking calls and Liz knew there were uniformed police out looking for Alex and Luke. It could have been her imagination but she had also heard a helicopter hover over the house for a few minutes before moving off. She had to resist the urge to get in her car and go and look for them herself.

All the activity seemed a comfort to her parents, who were sitting together on the sofa swapping memories of Luke.

Liz wanted to tell them to stop because their talk was lapsing into the past tense. She needed them to believe he was coming home. She couldn't force herself to think that later tonight Luke would be lying in his bed and this terrible time would just be a memory but she needed someone to think it, someone to believe it.

Alex could be five minutes away from the house. He could have been lying about the gun and he would just walk through the door and wonder what all the fuss was about.

She didn't know what would happen then. You couldn't charge someone with bringing a child home late. But maybe it was time to get a lawyer and to get the system involved. She wouldn't let this happen again. She bent her head and said a small prayer that she would get the chance to make that choice.

She watched Robert writing in his notebook. Suddenly this was very serious. Now no one would say to her, 'You're being hysterical and we're all going home.' She wanted them to take it seriously because the prickles along the back of her neck were sending her messages she didn't want to hear, but she also wanted them to fob her off. If they would just laugh at her she could relax, but here sat the two policemen like they had nothing better to do.

Dave came out of the kitchen and handed her a cup of hot sweet tea and Liz sipped at it. She hated sweet tea.

'Have you been a senior constable a long time?' she asked politely, as if they were at some social gathering.

Dave played along. 'Not long, only a couple of years now.'

Liz nodded and searched her brain for more questions to ask the nice-looking police officer with green eyes.

'Do you . . . do you have a family?'

'Well, no—I mean, yeah, I've got two sisters and my mum and dad, but I'm not married. I don't really get much time to, you know . . . date.'

Dave flushed and Liz felt a laugh coming on that she burned away with the tea.

Robert's phone rang again and Dave moved over to stand next to him while he had a whispered conversation without looking at Liz or her parents.

Liz felt her stomach contract as she watched Robert's face but then he ended the call and sat down again without saying anything. He wouldn't look at her. He looked at his shoes and Liz wondered what it was he had just heard.

There was no way he would keep news from her, would he? Not unless it was so bad they had to make sure they were right. Not unless . . . Liz took another sip of tea. She needed to think about cake. Luke liked sponge cake with chocolate icing. Her mother and Luke liked to bake together. Every time they baked Luke would end up covered from head to toe in cake batter and icing. Once he had even put the bowl on his head so he could lick out the last little bit. Ellen had had to sit down she was laughing so much.

If she had never had Luke Liz could see that she and her mother would have drifted to opposite ends of the world even though they lived only ten minutes apart. Each year she spent with Alex she had seen her mother less and less, and when she thought about it now she saw that Alex had encouraged her to hold on to childhood grievances. He had compared her mother checking out and into a whisky bottle for a few years to his mother leaving him. Liz had nodded during these discussions, feeling only a little disloyal to her mother. Her mother had never spent her time on the couch in an alcoholic stupor—well, not *never*. Mostly she had just never quite been there. Liz had been nursing her own issues with her father and the two of them had turned away from each other instead of towards healing together.

But when Luke had arrived Liz had needed her mother. Whatever her failings Ellen had seemed to know how to hold the baby and how to comfort him and when to worry enough to take him to the doctor. At first their conversations had only circled around Luke but eventually they had discussed other things. They still chafed at each other but Liz had known when she packed a bag that whatever her mother said, she would never say no to them staying.

Now whole evenings could pass where they just chatted without the edge of history. Luke had done that.

Luke, who liked to sing *Bob the Builder* songs and eat exactly one and a half slices of toast every morning. Luke, who put his arms around her and still smelled of baby shampoo. Luke, who was her baby boy and who might never come home again. Liz couldn't deal with the enormity of that fact. It wouldn't allow her to contain it. She was going mad trying to prepare herself.

She chewed on a nail again, despite the fact that at least three of her fingers were already bleeding.

'Look,' said Ellen, appearing in front of her, 'I think you need this, so just drink it.' She was holding a glass of whisky. In deference to Liz's taste she had added a touch of Coke. Liz took the drink and drank it down, enjoying the calming warmth. She held the glass out for a repeat.

'No,' said Ellen. 'Not now.'

Liz nodded, happy to have someone else in charge.

She looked at her watch. Alex was two hours and forty-seven minutes late. His phone had gone straight to voicemail the last few times she had called. The last twenty times she had called to be exact. The last call had been made from somewhere in this area but they couldn't find him and now his phone had been off for nearly an hour. He had been so close. If she had left the house and run to one of the nearby parks would she have found him? Where was he now? Where did you go with your son and a gun and your own fury?

The people in the house were starting to get jumpy. Rhonda had even cleaned up the kitchen with her mother. There was a sense of time passing more swiftly now. A sense that every minute counted. Alex was not standing on top of a building with the gun in one hand and Luke in the other but that was how it felt.

Robert didn't offer anyone tea. He didn't try to talk to any of them either, beyond asking questions that needed answers. He kept himself separate from them, unlike Dave, but Liz could see they had clearly defined roles in a situation like this. Robert's way of rubbing at the stubble on his chin and the knowing look that flicked across his face every time Alex's name was mentioned gave him the air of a seasoned professional. Dave was obviously much younger and Liz wondered how long he had been with the police. She imagined that in most situations Dave was probably the 'good cop'.

Liz had chewed all her fingernails and now she just felt numb. The situation was surreal. She remembered Molly telling her what it had been like to sit beside her dying mother a few months ago.

She had run into Molly when Luke was about a year old and they had taken a few steps towards each other and then just dropped back into their university friendship. They were giggling first-years again. They didn't discuss Alex. They talked about everything else but they never mentioned Alex. Molly never called her. Liz had never said anything but Molly seemed to understand. If she needed to get hold of Liz to change an arrangement she called Ellen and left a message. Ellen knew that Alex didn't like Molly and she also knew that Liz didn't like to make Alex angry.

'It's not normal to have to hide a friendship with a girlfriend, Liz. It's not like you're cheating on him,' said Ellen.

'Leave it alone, Mum,' said Liz as she had done so many times. As she had done so many, many times. 'It's just easier this way.'

She saw Molly during the day and she took care never to call her by her name when Luke began using words.

Molly had tried to explain to Liz what it was like to lose her mother and Liz had listened but she hadn't understood.

'It's like I'm sitting next to her bed and I know she's dying and I feel like I should be thinking all these profound things about how life is short and how much I love her and about all the wonderful things she has done for me, but all I'm thinking about is what to make for dinner and whether or not I watered the plants at home and fed the cat.'

Liz understood what she was saying now. The human mind had trouble coping with the big-picture stuff. Her son was missing and her husband was likely to do . . . what? But she couldn't think about that. She was thinking about mud cake and asking polite questions.

Dave came back over and pulled a chair up next to hers.

'They've got two helicopters in the air now and we've managed to track down the shopping centre he went to today. It was the big one near here so he was probably close by all day.'

Liz put her hand to her mouth. They had been nearby all

along. She should have left the house when he was five minutes late and started searching.

She closed her eyes and saw herself in the shopping centre—the same shopping centre where she and her mother had coffee this morning. She saw herself running through the centre and up the escalator and into the arcade by the movie theatre. She saw Luke standing by the Whack-a-Mole game that he loved and she reached out to him. She reached out to him and she grabbed him up and then she was running again, but this time she had Luke.

This time she had Luke.

She opened her eyes that were dripping again even though she felt dry inside. 'I should have gone to look for him. I should have known where Alex would take him.'

'He lives twenty minutes from here, Liz. You couldn't have known where he would go. We sent some constables over to Alex's house. It all looks pretty ordinary. It's neat and tidy and the cupboards are still full of clothes. I think he intends to go home. We just don't know when. We'll find him. We usually do.'

'What happens if you can't find him? What happens then?'

'We'll keep looking.'

'And if you never find them? What happens then?'

Dave looked down at his feet and Liz felt a little of his sorrow touch her. He didn't have an answer for her. There were probably women with vacant eyes and broken hearts who would know the answer. Liz didn't want to think about them.

15

Alex looked over at Luke. He was curled up on the front passenger seat with his thumb in his mouth. His blankie was covering his face. Alex didn't know how he could breathe.

Luke shouldn't have had a blankie anymore. Alex couldn't remember having a blankie when he was a kid. Liz was trying to keep Luke a baby when she should just have been having another baby instead.

She probably would have another baby one day, but maybe it would be with another man. A man who would move into Liz's life and start calling Luke 'son'.

Alex couldn't bear the thought of another man's hands on Liz's body. He couldn't bear it.

It was too late for Luke to still be sleeping but that didn't matter now. Nothing mattered now. 'Just bring him home, Alex. Nothing else matters now,' Liz had said.

He was just another thing that didn't matter to her. She made him feel like nothing, like dirt.

After he had spoken to his father he had switched the phone off for the last time. He had taken the battery out as well and dropped the whole thing on the floor and thought, 'Try tracking me now, you bastards.'

They did that now apparently. You saw it on all the cop shows.

She had called the police on him. Like he was some sort of criminal. If he took Luke back now he could see how it would all go down. They wouldn't be able to charge him with much because they didn't know about the gun, but Liz would get the courts involved and there would be a schedule and restrictions and every time he took the boy to the park he would be watched.

He and Liz would communicate through emails and lawyers and there would never be another dinner or another night when they could just be together and talk. Last night he had been overwhelmed with happiness. Her skin tasted like strawberries and her kisses tasted like wine. He didn't mind the extra weight on her butt even though he had called her fat when they were together. Last night he had loved every inch of her and he had been certain that it was only a matter of hours, maybe days, until he had his family back.

But she had asked him if he was crazy. She had told him they would never be together again. When she packed a suitcase and moved in with her mother she had abandoned him and now he knew she was never coming back.

He could move on and marry again but there would always be this fractured failure in his past and there would always be his son to remind him of his failure.

He looked over at his beautiful sleeping boy and smiled. They were so alike, the two of them. They both loved with all they had. They both loved Liz more than anything in the world, but he was broken because of that love. It was dangerous to love Liz too much.

He had to protect Luke from that. It was his job as a father. He had to protect Luke from having his heart broken like this. He didn't want his boy to ever have to feel this much pain.

Liz had taken his heart and stepped on it, grinding his feelings into dust. He knew that he would never be able to recover from this, never be able to move on with his life like she told him to. The pain was unbearable and he wanted it to end.

He got out of the car quietly so he wouldn't wake Luke and took the hose from the boot. It had been easy enough to research what to do on the internet. One night he had Googled the word just . . . just because. He'd had too much to drink and he was all alone in the house with his memories of the times when he had been able to make his wife and son happy.

There were so many sites on the internet, so many people in pain and so many ways to end that pain. There were chat rooms where people told each other to 'buck up' and that 'it was always darkest before the dawn' and other clichéd bullshit like that. Alex had had a bit of a laugh over that. He knew that none of the people on the internet felt the same way he did. None of them could have been in this much pain.

He had found out how to do it and he had put the hose in the boot. He liked having it there. It was a simple way to die really.

It would take a while because the car was a newer model but he had all the time in the world. It stretched before him now without the constraint of the passing hours. If Luke woke up he had a backup plan, but he didn't want to think about that yet.

He didn't know when the plan had begun to form.

Probably the day he came home and found the house empty.

Or the first time he had to drop Luke off after an afternoon in the park.

Or the day he had to tell people at work because they would call Liz's mobile when they couldn't get hold of him.

It could have been any one of those times really. And each time he was reminded of what had happened to his life he felt the wrongness of it. It just didn't seem possible.

On nights when he thought he was dying because his heart wouldn't stop racing and he couldn't get enough air into his lungs he would think about what he was going to do and it would calm him. He could relax and get to sleep then. He knew that eventually there would be an end to the pain and that gave him some peace.

Once, when he was thirteen, he had thought about doing it. Some bitch teacher had threatened to contact his father and tell him that Alex was skipping class and lying about it. He had felt so completely helpless to stop her, so out of control that he had not wanted to live anymore. He had taken his father's whisky and a box of Panadol into his room, intent on ending his life. He had mixed the whisky with some coke and started drinking and then he had begun to feel a little better and after he had gone through a quarter of the bottle he had passed out without even taking the pills. His father had been wildly pissed at him about the whisky and the lying bitch teacher had never even contacted him.

Now you could buy Panadol at any supermarket but he knew they wouldn't do the job. He had thought about using pills this time—proper sleeping pills—but he had understood that he could take the pills and drink until he passed out and it was possible that he would lie dead in the house for days before anyone tried to find him. He was more alone now than he had ever been. He didn't want to be a rotting corpse when they found him.

Liz would call only when she got pissed off that he hadn't come to pick up Luke and his father would call when he hadn't heard from him for a week or so but it would take awhile before people came to look for him instead of writing him off as being rude or busy.

He wanted them to find him. He wanted them to be sorry. He wanted Liz to be sorry. He would close his eyes and see Liz dressed in widow black with tears tracing their way down her face.

Last night he had gone home to bed and vowed to put the thought out of his mind. He hadn't washed the smell of her body away and he had slept so deeply, wrapped in the knowledge that they would be together again. But then she had ruined it all. She had lied again and she had used him and he was glad he had never taken the hose out of the boot and glad that he always carried his gun.

He knew that if she shed any tears it would not be for him. She would probably dance on his grave if she was given the chance, so he had to make sure that she was sad, sure that she shed tears. He had to make sure that she was devastated. It was what she deserved.

It was time now. He could feel it. He felt his mind grow still as he worked quietly to get the car ready. Originally he had only meant this for himself but he had always known that he could take his son with him. And now—after everything she had done—he knew that Luke had to come with him. He needed his son and his son needed him. It wasn't right that a father and son be separated.

Once the hose was connected to the exhaust pipe he wedged it into a window and made sure the rest of the car was sealed.

The thought crossed his mind that he should just push Luke out of the car. He could put him next to the road covered in his blankie and hope that someone else would find him, but he didn't like to think of what would happen if no one found him.

He started the car and relaxed in his seat.

The trouble was that Luke looked just like him. Same eyes, same nose, same chin. He was a little carbon copy of his father.

He was three now and just a cute kid but he would grow up and one day Liz would look at her son and see his father's face. Alex could see that happening and he could also see her turning against the boy. When Luke was a man his mother would hate him and Alex didn't want his boy to know that pain.

The car purred and he thought he felt a little sleepy but then he moved and he was wide awake again. How long was this supposed to take? He should have looked it up, but it wasn't like anyone who had succeeded had returned to report on the time it took to die.

He thought about Liz standing in front of two coffins. He felt the rightness of her suffering warm his heart. She had hurt him and in the future she would hurt her son the same way. She deserved to lose them both. She deserved to know the pain that he had felt. He wished that he could be around to see her suffer over losing her child but he was so sad and so tired he didn't want to have to deal with all of that.

Luke began to stir, to wake up, and Alex knew he couldn't let that happen.

The police were looking for them. He could hear helicopters in the distance, but that couldn't be for them, could it? They were well hidden anyway. Back here in the bush they were protected from prying eyes.

How long would this take?

'Dad,' said Luke and Alex looked over at his beautiful boy. He felt a moment of panic. Luke didn't like to sit still for too long. He would grow impatient in the car. He would get bored and cranky.

Alex closed his eyes and pretended to go to sleep. Maybe Luke would lie back down again. When he was still only a baby Alex had brought him to their bed before the sun was up. He didn't mind taking care of him in the mornings. Sometimes Luke would climb over him and stick his fingers in his ears and his nose, exploring everything, but sometimes he would lie down next to his father and drift off to sleep again.

'Daaad,' said Luke again, and Alex could hear his irritation.

It was no use, they didn't have the time. He needed Luke to be quiet, to sleep. It was a pity he wouldn't stay asleep. If he was awake he might try to get out of the car. He might throw a tantrum and get really difficult and then Alex would have to hit him and he really didn't want to have to hit him. Not now. Luke could be difficult sometimes but Alex had never laid a hand on him. He had never hurt his boy or made him feel afraid. Alex was proud of that. He was a good father. He knew he was a good father.

He would have to use the gun.

He opened the glove box and grabbed it, enjoying the heavy feel of it.

It had been surprisingly easy to get. He had a friend who knew someone who knew someone. It was the way these things worked.

'I'm moving to a crappy part of town so that I can keep the ex in jewellery,' he had told his friend. 'Bit worried about visitors in the night.' They had laughed together over what bitches women were and he had given his friend a couple of hundred dollars. The gun had come with six bullets and he had never bothered to try to get any more. He would only ever need one or two. He had known that.

Now he held it in his hands and released the safety catch while Luke looked on.

'Is that a gun, Dad?'

'Yes, my boy, it is.'

'Is it for real?'

'Yeah, it's for real.'

'Can I touch it?'

Alex looked at his son and his eyes filled with tears. It wasn't supposed to end like this. They were supposed to have been a family. In his future he had seen beach holidays and more children and a wife who loved him and never left. He was supposed to live a life different to the one his father had lived.

His father would be upset when he heard the news but Alex thought that it was possible he might understand as well. He knew the pain of losing the woman you loved. He knew what it was like to feel that no one cared about you. He knew what it meant to have your dreams shattered. He would understand.

'Dad,' said Luke again and Alex could hear the fear in the boy's voice. He knew something was wrong. He had seen a little too much in his life. Alex tried to keep himself from losing his temper while Luke was awake but of course there were times when Liz didn't care what her son saw.

Alex always made her explain to Luke the next day that it had just been a Mummy/Daddy fight and that she was fine and it meant nothing and Alex was a good dad and a good man. Luke needed to be able to trust his father.

'Listen to me, Luke. Listen carefully. I want you to do exactly what I tell you. You need to lie down and cover your head with your blankie.'

'But I'm not sleepy, Dad. I want to get up. I want to go home now. Mum said I can have pizza for dinner.'

'I know, Luke, I know you're not sleepy, but it's very important that you listen to me, okay? Can you do that for your dad, Luke? Can you do what I say just one last time?'

Alex knew that Luke was scared.

He was trying to keep his voice strong for his boy but he couldn't help the sadness that came bubbling out. Luke joined Alex in his tears and for a moment Alex thought that maybe he should just give all this up.

Luke wasn't crying the way he usually did. Usually he cried with the knowledge that any moment now his mother or father would make it all better but now the tears just slipped silently down his face.

Alex knew he could stop this right now. He could just throw the gun into the bushes. He could turn off the car and take the boy home. But it felt like it had gone too far.

He could feel his head beginning to spin a little.

How long was this supposed to take?

'Lie down now, Luke. Lie down and cover your head with your blankie.'

Luke gave him one last look, the appraising stare of a child, and Alex believed that he knew what was about to happen. He could have kicked and screamed or even tried to get out of the car but instead he just lay down on the seat and Alex could see his little body trembling. He put his thumb in his mouth and covered his head with his blankie and closed his eyes.

Alex sniffed, grateful for his acquiescence. Luke knew what was going to happen but he saw that it needed to be done. He saw the possibility of his future and he knew what it would be like so he lay down and closed his eyes and waited.

Alex lifted the gun and placed his finger on the trigger and he had a flash of a memory of the day Luke was born.

Liz had been in labour for fourteen hours and after Luke was born and everyone had left them alone she had made him promise to hold Luke while she slept and then she had just conked out. Her mother was on her way and so was Alex's father but at that moment it had just been him and his son, his firstborn child. The room was silent except for Liz's breathing. Luke's eyes were grey and even though he had screamed for his life the moment he was born now he was wrapped up tight and quiet.

Alex held him, still covered in some blood and that white stuff, and looked into his serious eyes and told him, 'I will never let anyone hurt you—never.'

It felt like yesterday that he had been that father at the very beginning of a perfect life. He looked over at the beautiful boy he had promised to take care of for the rest of his life. He touched his silky hair and felt the small body tremble.

He lifted the cold heavy gun and pointed it. It would be quick and painless and then there would be no more pain for either of them. He reached back and picked up the small pillow he had brought from the house.

It was one of those silly little pillows embroidered with the words *Home Sweet Home*.

He didn't want to hear the sound.

He didn't want to see what the gun would do.

'Dad,' said Luke quietly, and Alex could hear the fear in his little boy's voice.

He didn't reply. There was nothing left to say.

Three hours and ten minutes late

'Oh Jesus,' said Julie. 'Oh God, Aiden, we're too late. Oh God, the poor kid.'

'Check for signs of life, Julie,' said Aiden. His voice was loud and firm.

Julie's hands were shaking. She checked once and then twice and then she shook her head and brushed away the tears.

Aiden checked the body on his side of the car.

Both bodies were still warm in the crisp late afternoon air.

'I just can't believe it,' said Julie to Aiden over and over again.

Aiden put his hand up so she would keep quiet and he called it in.

'Send a bus,' he said. 'Send two.'

Lisa at the station took the call and he heard her sharp intake of breath when he told her they would need the ambulances.

Lisa had taken the first call from the mother. Lisa had done everything right and then they had all done everything right and still here they were in this park in the almost-dark with the car and the bodies.

They had done everything right.

Julie sank to her knees and put her head in her hands. She had only just been made a full constable. She carried pictures of her nieces in her wallet. She stopped to talk to kids on the street and she bent down to their level so they wouldn't find her scary.

Aiden could believe it. He looked at the blood-covered bodies and he could believe it.

He had never seen anything like it before but he had mates who'd been on this kind of case and they told tales at the pub. They drowned out the images with one too many beers.

He looked around the empty park and watched the swing move in the slight wind that was picking up.

Everyone would be here soon. The ambulances would come and there would be more police.

The park would fill with flashing lights and the neighbours would stand outside peering at someone else's tragedy, careful not to get too close. Families always stood huddled together—grateful to be standing in a group, grateful that no one was missing.

If he listened beyond the quiet of this park he could already hear the scream of ambulance sirens and the whine of more police cars. The lights had come on and they lit up the empty oval, throwing shadows over the car.

Aiden had wanted the car to be empty. He had wanted the guy to be taking a bushwalk with his kid, but there they were. They were both in the front seat. The boy had a blue blanket over his face but the blood was in his hair. The blood was all over the blanket. He wanted to touch the little body but it was important that nothing was moved. Forensics would be along any minute.

There was no one else in the park and Aiden was thankful for that. The last thing he needed to deal with was some traumatised member of the public.

A park was a place for a child to play.

The little boy might have been looking forward to climbing the ladder and whizzing down the slide. He might have anticipated the sweet stomach-turning feel of flying through the air on the swing. He might have wanted to have a go at the climbing frame even though it looked a bit complicated.

Aiden didn't like to think what he would have felt when he realised that today he was not allowed to play in the park. That he was never going to play in the park again.

They'd all hoped it would end differently.

But the reality of a situation like this was that they never made it on time.

There were too many stories around with this kind of ending.

Last-minute rescues only happened in the movies. In the movies, some hero got to rush in and rescue the kid, and then everyone got to have a laugh at the pub later on. If you watched too much television you could end up believing that the police were all-powerful, that nothing was ever left unsolved and that it was never too late. Children tended not to die on television. It was bad for ratings.

They died in real life.

In real life the police were mostly too late.

The sirens got closer. They sounded more desperate now.

The media would have heard they'd found the car. There was no way to keep the buggers off the channel. Today they would have reasoned that they were already involved. They would have been listening in and waiting. Aiden had never met a journalist who was afraid of biting the hand that fed him. In fact they seemed to relish the idea.

They tapped into mobile phones and used computers whenever they could. It was rumoured that one of the majors had hired someone whose only job was to hack into police phones, police computers and police radio.

With a bit of luck backup would get here first and section off the park so all the cameras would get were a few shots of serious-looking police officers shaking their heads.

Someone would already be preparing a statement to read once the wife had been told.

They would have to erect a tent to bring out the bodies.

The editors would have a field day with this. They loved a good family tragedy. They would find themselves a bunch of experts and interest groups and criticise the system as though anything could have prevented this.

You couldn't possibly legislate enough to cover what people did when they were motivated by anger and hate and probably humiliation.

Or by some twisted concept of love.

He didn't know all the facts but that's what this would be about. It always was.

His first day on the job, one of the detectives had told a group of them, 'It's either sex, which is all bound up with love, or it's money, boys and girls. Not much else motivates your average human being.'

Aiden had smiled with everyone else, feeling only slightly alarmed by the jaded comment. But that was a few years ago, and now he said the same thing to every new recruit he came across. It helped when you needed to ask questions.

He wiped his eyes, telling himself, 'Buck up, matey—you've seen shit like this before.'

But there was so much blood. Blood smelled like metal. He had been a cop for four years before he'd seen enough blood to know that. There was so much of it inside the car the smell set his teeth on edge.

The grass underfoot was wet and the air was changed by the houses with wood-burning fires but the metallic stench surrounded the car.

The cold was taking hold but the bodies in the car were still warm.

They'd opened the windows and doors, careful not to dislodge the hose. The bastard had covered every angle. Aiden had used gloves and angled his body inside to turn off the engine.

There was no way this man was letting either of them get out alive.

They had come so close to saving them, so fucking close.

They were five minutes from the house where the mother lived. Only five minutes. There was a whole scary world out there but the most grisly of murders usually took place in the kitchen. People spent their lives looking out for suspicious strangers when the strangest person was usually the one sharing your bed.

They would have missed the car if he hadn't insisted on pulling over and checking out the bushes. What was that? Dumb luck? Police instinct? God?

At least the mother would know now, sometimes the not-knowing could be a lot worse but, who would want to know a thing like this? His heart sank in sympathy with the woman. He could see the night she had ahead of her. Hopefully someone would get a doctor and he would knock her out until she could cope with what was coming.

They would have to get themselves together. Everyone would be here soon.

'Buck up, matey,' he said again.

He walked over to the car again and peered at the two figures inside.

'Who will go and tell the family?' asked Julie. She had come to stand next to him. She was wiping her face, getting ready for the circus.

'Williams and Mathieson are there with the mother now. They'll get the call so maybe they'll tell her—or they might decided to wait for a social worker. Depends if they think they can control the situation or not.'

They stared down at the bodies as the sirens got closer and closer. There were a couple of people coming out of their houses now. The park would be full soon. This was better than television.

Aiden leaned into the car again to see where the gun had dropped. He couldn't see it and decided that it must have fallen under the seat.

Later, when he was recounting the story to his young wife, who would sit through it all with her face a mask of horror, he didn't mention how glad he had been to have Julie standing next to him when the world shifted just a little and one of the bodies in the car moved.

One of them moved.

Julie had blue eyes and blonde hair and Aiden's wife didn't need to know that afterwards, at the pub, they had hugged for just a little longer than they should have done.

He was glad Julie was standing next to him because even though they had checked and rechecked and there were no signs of life one of them moved and let out a sound that was more animal than human.

He had nearly lost it but Julie sprang into action and the bus arrived one minute later.

'Bastard,' whispered Julie as the ambos worked on him.

'I checked him twice—more than twice,' Julie said to the medic.

'It can be difficult to find a pulse sometimes,' said the medic.

Out came the oxygen mask and the towels so they could wipe away the blood.

The medics moved in slow motion, dancing around the body and finally getting a proper response. They nodded seriously to each other. Aiden looked around the park, noting the slow movement of people towards the ambulance.

'Shit,' he said.

'Time to go,' said the woman who was driving.

Together the paramedics lifted the stretcher into the ambulance.

'I'm going with you,' said Julie.

'Okay,' said the man, whose name was Christian.

'Why?' asked the woman with *Linda* on her tag.

'I don't want to let him out of my sight,' said Julie. 'I need to watch him.'

'Whatever,' said Christian, 'let's just get to the hospital—Julie, is it?'

'Yeah,' said Julie. 'Do you think he's going to be okay?'

'I can't answer that question. Right now he's breathing. He's still warm so it can't have been long.'

'Will he be okay?'

'You know I can't answer that question.'

Julie nodded her head. She understood that they were not allowed to say anything. Only a doctor could tell her but she had asked the question anyway.

'How does stuff like this happen?' she said.

Christian looked at her and shrugged his shoulders.

'Yeah,' said Julie. 'It's a bit like that.'

It had only been three hours.

Three hours didn't seem like enough time to change the world but Julie knew well enough that it only took minutes for a life to alter so drastically that a person couldn't imagine ever being the same again.

She was aware that when it came to all the terrible things a human mind could think up, three hours was practically a lifetime.

16

Robert's phone and Dave's both began ringing. The noise sliced through the mostly silent room.

The discordant sounds heralded the news they had been waiting for. Without any more information, Liz sensed the end in the rings.

The policemen moved away from the living room and into the kitchen. Liz stood up from her chair and began walking after them. They closed the door to the kitchen firmly.

She stood just a few feet away and thought about kicking it down. The calls could only mean one thing. They had found them.

She could put her ear against the door and hear everything. When her parents were still together they had always argued in the kitchen. With her ear pressed to the door Liz had been able to hear her father's part in the discussion trail off a little more with each passing week. Eventually it was only her mother's voice that came through the door, whining, arguing and needling, and Liz had known that her father was gone already.

She wrapped her arms around herself and stared at the door, unable to make out what was going on. Robert was speaking now but all he was saying was 'yep' and 'no' and 'fine'.

Everyone else in the room was silent, all of them staring at the closed kitchen door.

'It's probably just an update,' said Rebecca.

'Yeah,' agreed Rhonda. 'You know it's all just about keeping the red tape running. They're just reporting back. It's okay, Liz. Sit down.'

But even Rebecca didn't sound convinced. There were no more positives in this situation.

'It's dark and it looks so cold outside,' said Liz. 'Luke needs his big jacket when it's cold. You know, Mum—the one with the fleece hood. He needs that jacket.'

Ellen stood up from the couch and she walked over to where Liz was standing. She reached out and touched her shoulder but Liz gave a little shrug and stepped away.

'I know the jacket,' said Ellen softly.

'Will you get it, Mum?' said Liz. Her back was to the room.

Ellen turned to look at Jack, who shrugged.

'Okay, sweetie, I'll get it. I'll just go to his room and get it.'

Liz nodded.

In her head the theme to *Bob the Builder* went round and round. Bob could fix it—yes he could.

Robert and Dave came out of the kitchen.

Ellen returned holding Luke's jacket.

Robert looked at the roomful of people and then into Liz's eyes. 'Just an update,' he said, but then he looked at the door and walked away to the other end of the room. Dave didn't say anything but he too looked towards the door. They were waiting for something.

Both policemen sat away from everyone else.

Liz watched them for a moment and then she gave her body a small shake and turned back to her chair. She picked up the phone and dialled Alex's mobile one more time. Each time she dialled she imagined that this might be the time he picked up and that she would find the right words. Now she dialled the number her fingers could trace without her even looking and she watched the policemen.

They would not meet her eyes. She could have simply pressed Alex's name on her mobile phone but each time she called him she pressed each number, hoping that this time the universe would have the time to get the outcome right.

Later she would look at her mobile and see that she had called him two hundred and fifty times.

'I think you need to rest a little, Liz,' said Rhonda.

Everyone in the room nodded.

The room was filling up with the silent contemplation of people waiting for the worst. When everyone had arrived there had been a distinct feeling that the time needed to pass, and that once enough time had passed they could all look back at those hours and agree that it had been difficult. They could remember their concern but they could also shake their heads and thank whoever they needed to thank that everything was fine. In a few years they would probably be able to laugh at how worried they had all been and it had all been over something silly.

Now the possibility that these few hours were just the beginning was all anyone could think. There would be no sighs of relief, no 'how silly we were'.

He didn't need a gun. Luke was just a little boy. His third birthday had only been a month ago. On his cake dinosaurs had roamed an iced green landscape and there was one extra unlit candle on the side—to grow on. The weather had been warmer then and Liz had invited his whole preschool class and some of the children from his old playgroup.

She had made jelly shapes and clown cupcakes. Jack had paid for an entertainer and Spiderman had come to play games and make balloon animals. Luke had whooped and shouted and jumped through the day. That night she had snuggled him into bed and he had put his little hands on her cheeks and said, 'That was the bestest day of my whole entire life, Mum.'

'It was the bestest day of my life too, Lukie,' she had replied and then he had gripped his blankie and put his thumb in his mouth.

Liz and her mother had been cleaning up well into the night but they had discussed the other mothers and laughed about Spiderman falling over and all the children jumping on top of him. Alex had come but he had been quiet and stayed off to one side for most of the party. Luke hadn't wanted to be with his father when the other children were there to play with and Liz had felt a small stab of sympathy for how out of place he looked. She had wanted to go over and talk to him but Ellen had told her that Alex needed to get used to this. Liz was still holding him off then, still being distant and cold, and so she had ignored him and enjoyed the party. She wondered now if he had been planning this even then. If she had shown him some kindness, would he have abandoned the plan?

It was inconceivable that there would never be another birthday. Inconceivable that Luke would never crawl into her bed at the crack of dawn and ask serious questions about space. It was not the way this day should have ended.

Liz walked back and forth across the living room. Her father's chair had ceased to be a comfort. Her skin itched and her heart raced.

'Please, Liz,' said Ellen. 'Just sit down and close your eyes for a few minutes.'

'I can't rest. He has my baby. I can't . . . I just don't know what to do. Can you tell me what to do?' she said, looking at Robert.

Robert stood up and drew a breath, then sat down again, shaking his head sadly.

It was then that Liz knew for sure what the phone call had been about.

His expression was blank but his eyes held the telltale shine of unshed tears. Robert knew the truth but he was keeping it to himself. Perhaps he knew what would happen if he said the words and he was worried about how to handle things or maybe he was waiting for final news, final words, so that he could tell her where her baby was.

'How long do I have?' she wondered. 'How many more minutes of hope do I have left?'

•

Robert rubbed at his face and then stood up and made his way to the kitchen. Dave followed.

'We need to get the social worker here,' whispered Dave.

'I know,' said Robert. 'I've called her.'

'Maybe you should just tell her. Tell her and put her out of her misery.'

'Dave, there's a proper way to do these things. We have to wait for the paramedics to confirm death at the scene before we say anything. We can't have everyone screaming down there and getting in the way. It's a crime scene.'

'Fuck, I can't believe this has happened. I can't believe we've been here for hours and we still couldn't stop this from happening.'

'Mostly we can't stop it, Dave. Mostly we just pick up the pieces.'

'I can't believe how close he was,' said Dave.

The door to the kitchen moved a little and even though both men registered the movement, they didn't understand that Liz had pressed her ear against the wood, desperate for an answer.

'They'd searched the park already. I think Aiden was the one who pushed to go back. Who knows how long he's been there.'

Outside the door Robert heard Liz say, 'Oh, oh God,' and then they both heard the front door slam.

'Shit,' said Robert.

'We have to stop her,' said Dave as they moved out of the kitchen.

In the living room the women stood looking at each other.

'She's gone,' said Ellen. 'She's gone. What did you say?' she shouted. 'What did you say? Where's my grandson?'

The words were shouted at the air because Dave and Robert were already running. The park was so close. They were running and even though Dave was fast he couldn't catch up with Liz, who was running on her fear and despair and her knowledge that it was all over. Right now it was all over.

17

'So what?' said Rhonda

'Where?' said Jack.

'The park,' said Ellen. 'It's the only place close enough. It has to be the park. That's where she was going, it's the park. We have to get to the park, Jack. I can't run, Jack. We have to get to the park.'

'Well move, woman,' said Jack. 'Just move.'

Rhonda and Rebecca dashed outside to Rebecca's car. 'We'll follow you,' she shouted at Ellen.

Ellen didn't say anything. She slid into Jack's car, noting that it was new and plush. She was holding Luke's coat. 'It's cold,' she thought. 'He'll be so cold.'

Jack screeched out of the driveway.

Ellen watched the houses merge into one as Jack sped down the street.

It was Saturday night and there would be families getting ready to go out together and parents making sure the babysitter was coming. Ordinary families living ordinary lives had no idea that in their neighbourhood, on their street, there was something so completely extraordinary going on that when the news spread, sliding through the television sets and computers, they would look out of their windows and know that their walls had been breached. If they could live near such a thing and not know it was there, what hope was there for them?

Ellen had not been looking forward to pizza with Luke and Liz but she hadn't been able to think of a reason why she couldn't join them.

Now she knew she would give anything, *anything*, to be getting ready to brave the noisy pizza restaurant where they didn't serve alcohol.

'We long for lives filled with drama and excitement,' she thought, 'but when it comes we can only desire the routine and the mundane, because in the moments that bore us with their repetition we can at least be sure that we are safe.'

She needed another drink. She desperately needed to feel the burn.

This was happening. This was really happening.

This morning Luke had showed her how many Cheerios he could fit into his mouth. He had made it to twenty before he had to spit the whole lot out. She should have scolded him for the mess but it was so funny she had just laughed. She was glad now that she had laughed.

She was glad that she had given him an extra chocolate treat last night even though Liz had said he'd had enough. She was glad she had let him crawl into her bed some nights when he felt like company and Liz had told him not to wake her. She should have hugged him more, read him more stories, played more games, but she knew that now was not the time for her pain. Now she would need to be a mother to her devastated child and only later, when she was alone, could she take out her grandmother pain and embrace it.

'We're here, baby, we're right here,' whispered Ellen to herself. 'Right here,' said Jack.

•

Liz ran. She pumped her arms and legs and she ran because she could not be there fast enough. Her breath was ragged and she felt her nose run and eyes water but she couldn't stop. She was barefoot. 'When did I take off my shoes?' she thought and then her foot was pinched by a sharp pain that she knew would bleed, but she could not stop.

He was so close. Had he been there all along? Was the arcade a lie? Or had he gone to the park only when he knew what he was going to do? Had he been planning this all day?

Even as she ran and her body began to sweat, Liz could feel how cold it was getting. 'Did he let him have his blankie?' she thought. His blankie would have kept him warm. He would have been terrified without his blankie. He would have cried.

'He would have cried for me,' she thought, and the pain in her foot was cancelled out by the sharp agony in her heart. He would have cried for me.

She wanted to stop. She could see the park up ahead and she wanted to stop because the red and blue lights flashing in the sky could only mean one thing. She forced her legs to go faster. 'How long do I have left?' she thought. How long before I am sure of what has happened to my son? She would not be able to live without him. In the rush of her heartbeat and the burn of her lungs she was completely sure of that and the thought was a comfort.

It made perfect sense that Alex had chosen the park. Alex loved the park. It wasn't a big park and the equipment was old and in need of upgrading but it was their park. It was the park he had taken her to after their first date because he hadn't wanted to drop her home and end the night.

'I know where we can go,' she had said and then she had directed him to the park near her mother's house.

They'd kissed and Alex had held her face like she was the most beautiful thing he'd ever seen.

It was the first place they had made love. Alex had brought a blanket and they had hidden themselves amongst the trees and bushes. It had been very late at night in the middle of summer and they had been completely alone.

'One day, we'll have our own house and we won't have to sneak around like this,' Alex had said when they were lying together and looking at the stars.

The second day after they brought Luke home from the hospital Alex had made her get up and get dressed.

'We'll take our boy to see our park,' he told her, and then they had parked at her mother's house and walked.

'The air will do you good,' he had said and he had been right. They had walked carefully, pushing the shiny new pram, and Liz had looked at the world that was different only because she was different and Alex had smiled and smiled. 'This is our family park now,' he had said. 'We are now a family. You and me and Luke.'

And of course she had laughed with delight at the wonderfulness of it all. It had always been their park. There were parks closer to their house and parks where the equipment was new but they had always come back to this park.

It was where Luke had learned to climb and how to move a swing. It was where he had fallen over and scraped his knee and howled at the injustice of a body that wouldn't quite do what he told it to. It was the park where they had become a family—and now?

What was it now?

Three hours and forty minutes late

'Let's go, Linda,' said Christian, and the ambulance began to move slowly.

The park had filled up with people summoned by the flashing lights and the promise of drama.

'Come on,' muttered Linda, 'get out of the way; you've seen whatever there was to see.' She tooted the horn once.

Julie closed her eyes, wondering how this was all going to go down, wondering about the woman waiting for news of her husband and son, and then she heard a scream echo across the park.

The agonising scream filled the air. Julie stood up and looked out of the back doors. At first she couldn't see anything but then

Linda made a slow turn and Julie saw a woman running across the park. She was waving her arms and screaming for all she was worth. Her long black hair was blowing over her face and her feet were bare. She was moving fast but also doing some sort of hop and limp.

'She must be hurt,' thought Julie.

The woman kept going until she virtually bumped into the ambulance. In the park Julie watched people move back from the strange shrieking creature.

Julie knew that this was the woman who had been waiting for news. This was the woman who'd made the first call and the second call and who had summoned the police and this was the woman whose life was about to be shattered.

'Stop,' said Julie.

'No,' said Linda.

'Just fucking stop, okay. This must be her.'

'We have to get to the hospital,' said Linda.

Behind the woman were Robert and Dave. Robert looked ready for a heart attack but Dave was a runner and he looked like he was just out for a stroll. He hadn't been able to catch the woman though.

Linda continued to move the bus slowly until there was a bang on the side. Robert had hit the side.

'Stop,' he shouted and it was an order.

'Fuck,' said Linda. She stopped and Julie stood up to open the doors.

The woman looked into the ambulance. Her eyes and nose were streaming.

'Where's my son?' she said.

•

Jack spun his wheels into the park where Ellen could see two ambulances with their red and blue lights turning frantic circles. There were no sirens but the park was filled with numerous police cars. And people, so many people just standing and watching.

'Fucking vultures,' thought Ellen. She jumped out of the car and pushed herself across the park towards the ambulances. A policeman stepped in front of her to try and stop her from getting to the ambulance with the back doors open.

'It's my daughter,' she screamed and then she saw Jack's arm shoot out and push the man away.

She stopped just short of the ambulance. Inside Liz was standing with a policewoman and looking down at the stretcher. And she was howling. Liz was howling and Ellen felt her body begin to fall.

'No you don't,' said Jack, grabbing her from behind.

'She needs us now, El, she needs us and we will be there. Breathe deep, luv. Here we go.'

•

Inside the ambulance Liz was looking down at her son, her boy, her blood-soaked little man, and she could not make the howling stop.

She wanted it to be silent.

In the moment he was born everything stopped. It was only for long enough to take a breath but everything stopped. The midwife was quiet and the doctor just breathed. No machines beeped and the noises outside were absorbed by the miracle in the room. Her child greeted the world in silence. She needed silence again now so that he could farewell it.

She turned to find her mother to ask her to help stop the noise and she touched her face as she turned and it was then that she realised that she was making the noise. She was an animal mourning the loss of her young and she had no idea how to stop herself from tearing her hair and clothes.

The policewoman stepped in front of her and grabbed her face with both hands, just as Luke liked to grab her face.

'It was the bestest day of my life, Mum.'

She turned Liz's face towards her and their eyes locked. Liz had never seen such blue eyes.

'No,' said the policewoman firmly.

'No,' she said again in a loud voice.

'Look,' she said. She grabbed Liz's hand and placed it on his chest. Liz pulled away as if she had touched fire.

His face was covered in an oxygen mask and she wondered why they had bothered.

'Look,' said the policewoman again. This time she held Liz's hand on his little chest and even though Liz wanted to pull away and run and run forever she kept her hand there.

And then she felt it.

It was a small movement. It was so small and so light she could have imagined it, but she watched as her hand moved up and down with his chest.

'It's not his blood,' said the policewoman. 'It's not his blood. Do you understand?'

Liz nodded, keeping her hand on his chest.

'But what?' she said.

'Carbon monoxide poisoning,' said the man sitting at Luke's head.

Liz looked up and saw him for the first time. He was watching the oxygen tank.

'He's not going to die,' said the man. 'With new cars it takes a lot longer before it gets critical.'

'He's not going to die,' repeated the police officer.

'He's not going to die,' said Liz.

The tears in her eyes were matched by those running down the policewoman's face.

He wasn't going to die.

18

Liz wanted to stroke his head but she couldn't bear to touch the blood. On his fine hair it looked fake and gluggy. It could have been paste and food colouring. It could have been red paint darkened with brown.

But it was Alex's blood. Because it could have been nothing else.

Liz lay her cheek gently on Luke's chest and felt him breathe. She looked out of the ambulance to see her parents. Jack was shaking hands with another policeman and Robert and Dave were on their phones. The air was charged with relief. It crackled around the park and bounced along through the crowd.

'We need to get him to the hospital,' said the policewoman in the ambulance.

Liz felt Luke's little chest move up and down.

'He's alive,' she said.

'Yes, he is,' said the man. 'He's strong.'

As the three of them watched, Luke's arm rose and fluttered near his face.

'He keeps doing that,' said the man. And his voice told Liz that Luke's butterfly hand was not a good sign.

'Why is it happening?' said Liz.

The man looked down at his machine.

'Why, tell me what that means.' She looked at the policewoman who was looking at the paramedic. There was something they didn't want to say. Something important.

'The ER doc will take a look at him. Don't worry about anything now. Let's just get him there,' he said.

'But . . .' said Liz as she remembered something she had read or seen or heard. 'Brain damage,' she almost shouted. 'That's what you're worried about, isn't it? You're worried about brain damage. From the carbon monoxide? That's what it is, isn't it?'

The man looked at Luke and busied himself with checking his oxygen mask.

'Just tell me, please,' said Liz.

'We'll let the doc take a look, okay?' Liz looked at him and caught the look of resignation on his face. His nametag identified him as 'Christian'.

Liz nodded. He would not give her any answers now.

Luke's hand floated up and down again, dancing to his own special music.

The brain was a secret the body kept and Liz could see that this simple action possibly told a tale of a long recovery. His body wasn't listening to his brain. Unless of course he meant to make the movement.

Luke's arm floated up again and this time it connected with the mask on his face and pushed at it.

'Maybe he wants to talk or something,' said Liz. Inside her chest her heart swelled with the greatest of hopes. The hope only a mother can hold.

Christian looked at her sadly. 'I don't think so.'

Luke's hand batted the mask again and this time he moaned as well.

The paramedic leaned forward and lifted the mask away from Luke's face and then, in the silent ambulance in the fading light, they heard him speak.

His eyes remained closed and his voice was low and came out slowly as his throat found a way to work.

'I want my pizza, Mum. I want pizza with olives.'

His body relaxed again, he had said what he needed to say and his arm drifted down by his side.

Christian smiled at Liz and Liz could see his eyes shine.

'Well, that's bloody marvellous,' he said. 'Bloody marvellous.'

Julie the policewoman smiled and Liz smiled back at her and then Liz felt a laugh bubble up in her throat. She caught it behind her teeth, embarrassed under the circumstances, but Julie leaned forward and squeezed her hand.

'Much more where that came from,' she said.

Liz nodded and held on to Luke's hand. His little fingers curled slightly, holding right back.

No one mentioned Alex. In the middle of this miracle his name would not be spoken and Liz washed away any thought of him. There would be time to think it through, time to work out what had happened and plenty of time, endless reserves of time, to ask why. But now she would not think about him.

'It's time to go now,' said Christian, and Julie stood up and started to close the doors.

The ambulance began to move slowly again. Outside Liz could see her mother turn and move towards them.

'Wait,' said Ellen, trying to climb in, 'I'll come too.'

'Sorry, ma'am,' said Christian cheerfully. 'Only the mother.'

'I'm still a mother,' thought Liz. 'Still a mother.'

Liz felt a laugh bubble up in her throat again. The rush of emotions was making her giddy. She breathed slowly in and out and tried to calm herself.

She was still a mother.

'Pack a bag for us, Mum,' she called to Ellen.

'I will,' said Ellen. 'Dad and I will be right behind you. We'll get everything from the house and meet you there.'

'Pack his Bob the Builder pyjamas and some stuff for him to play with. You know what he likes.'

'Yes,' said Ellen. 'I know what he likes.'

'And, Mum . . .'

'Yes?'

'Don't forget a new blankie. He needs his blankie.'

Epilogue

'Luke, can you please stop jumping up and down?' said Liz.

'When's P'liceman Dave coming, Mum, when, when, when, when?'

'Luke, please stop. I need to get this sunscreen on you or we're not going to the lake.'

'P'liceman Dave says I'm gonna fish—I'm gonna fish and I'm gonna catch a big fish and then he says we gotta frow it back.'

'It's "policeman", Luke. Can you say "policeman"?' said Ellen, coming into the kitchen. 'I'll do this, Liz. Go and finish getting ready.'

'God, he's like a mad creature today,' said Liz.

'He's just excited.'

'Yes, well, we're all excited when Policeman Dave comes over,' laughed Liz.

She made her way to her box-filled bedroom.

Now she was counting down the days to moving home. Now the safety of her mother's house was beginning to suffocate. Now she longed for the silence of her own space.

She and Luke were finally ready to face their empty house. There was new paint and a new carpet, even though the old ones had been perfectly good.

'Start fresh,' her father had said, and then he had painted over memories and changed the way everything looked with new carpet. Liz had stood in the centre of the room and couldn't quite place Alex anywhere in the house. He didn't belong there anymore.

'Do you want me to get rid of his stuff?' her father had asked.

'Yes,' replied Liz, but then, 'No.'

'I need to keep some stuff for Luke, Dad. I need to keep some stuff for his son.'

The box she kept held only the best memories, only the keepsakes that could not damage Luke.

In a week's time they would move. Her father and her mother would come and help and so would Molly and Rhonda and Rebecca and some of the other women from the group. Liz visited occasionally now but she was in a different space to the women in the group. She could no longer nod her head in time with theirs.

Liz had wanted to protest that she didn't need anyone's help to move but those words did not sit comfortably with her anymore. She needed everyone's help. She could not face this alone and she knew there was no need for her to do so. She called her parents for advice and asked her friends for help and listened to her psychologist.

At Alex's funeral she had held on to her parents while Frank stared at a point above her head. He had lost his only child and, standing opposite him, Liz had not wanted to think about the possibility that she could have lost her only child as well.

They should have been bonded by the loss but Liz's tears touched her lips with the salty taste of relief and Frank's off-centre gaze held only accusation. He had not come up to her when it was all over. Her father had squared his shoulders and dared the man to approach.

Luke was not there, which everyone had agreed was for the best. Liz was grateful he would not have to see his father's body being lowered into the ground. The sound of freshly turned soil hitting the wood forced a sob from her lips. He had chosen the wine and told her he loved her and begged her not to leave.

Luke wanted to know what had happened. Even though he remembered nothing he suspected something large as he surveyed the endless gifts that just kept coming. Once the news floated through the air, even strangers breathed in Liz's joy at her son's escape. They sent books and teddy bears which Luke declared were 'for babies'.

There were three new blankies in the cupboard to replace the one that had covered Luke and soaked up his father's blood.

The psychologist said it would take time. 'Time and patience and a lot of love,' she said.

'No problem there,' said Liz.

The world moved on and there were new words and ideas every day, but still 'a lot of love' seemed to be the solution for most things.

Luke thought the psychologist was a kind lady who liked to play games with him. Luke thought Policeman Dave came to play with him.

'Maybe we should tell him a little bit of the truth,' Ellen had said.

'It will change who he is,' said Liz. So they waited and said nothing, although Liz wrote it all down for him and one day she would give him the words that were still fresh, with memory and fear and heartache, and help him work his way through the truth.

'What happened to Dad?' he would ask every now and again.

'He had an accident and he's gone to live in heaven,' was the reply they had all agreed on.

Liz sometimes looked ahead to a rebellious teenage Luke who would accuse her of driving his father away, of not loving the man enough, of being a bad wife. She welcomed the idea of a tall Luke who towered over her because at least she would have the chance to see it now. She would cope with whatever he threw at her.

Liz was prepared to accept her part in it all but could only be relieved at how it had all worked out. She would never know what stopped Alex using the gun on Luke but she would remain forever grateful. Forever grateful.

She had found a small piece of her love for him that she held on to and used to keep his memory positive for Luke.

Outside she heard a car door slam and knew that Dave had arrived. She stood brushing her hair and heard the doorbell ring and Luke talk about fish and sunscreen and the chocolate ice cream he had been promised.

It was just an ordinary day and they would join other families on the lake and Liz would be bothered by the flies and Luke would get irritating when he was tired and Dave would try to keep them both calm and happy because as far as Liz could tell that seemed to be his only agenda.

But sometime during the day, maybe right in the middle, Liz would close her eyes and remember that this was a future that might not have been.

She would take herself back to those hours and she would remember her certainty that her life was over.

And then she would open her eyes and say no to another ice cream and share a sandwich with Dave and watch the boats.

'Hey, Mum,' said Luke.

'Hey Mum, hey Mummy, Mummy Mum, Mum,' said Luke.

Acknowledgements

Many thanks, once again, to Ali Lavau for her editing expertise.

To Karen Ward for answering all my questions and helping me through the process.

To Jane Palfreyman for her patience and support.

As always to Gaby Naher, who reads and rereads and then reads again.

To my mother, Hilary, who is my beta reader, babysitter, counsellor and coffee date and who found a nice way to say, 'You need to start again.'

And finally to David, Mikhayla, Isabella and Jacob. There is no need to yell, dear family, I'm always in the loft.

If you are feeling distressed and need to talk to someone imme-diately, the following telephone counselling services are available 24 hours, 7 days:

Lifeline—13 11 14
Suicide Call Back Service—1300 659 467
MensLine Australia—1300 78 99 78

You can also talk to your local GP or health professional.
 If you would like some more general information about mental health or other services, you can contact the following:

SANE Australia—www.sane.org or 1800 18 SANE
(1800 18 7263)

beyondblue: the national depression initiative—
www.beyondblue.org.au or 1300 BB INFO (1300 22 4636)

Lifeline service finder (for local contacts)—
www.lifeline.org.au